T0166487

WITH THE ANIMALS

Originally published in French as *Rapport aux bêtes* by Gallimard, Paris, 2002
Copyright © Éditions Gallimard, Paris, 2002
Translation copyright © 2012 by W. Donald Wilson
First edition, 2012
All rights reserved

Library of Congress Cataloging-in-Publication Data

Revaz, Noëlle.
[Rapport aux bétes. English.]
With the animals / Noelle Revaz ; translated by W. Donald Wilson. -- 1st ed.
  p. cm.
"Originally published in French as Rapport aux bétes by Gallimard, Paris, 2002."
ISBN 978-1-56478-754-5 (pbk. : alk. paper) -- ISBN 978-1-56478-721-7 (cloth : alk. paper)
I. Wilson, William Donald, 1938- II. Title.
PQ2678.E8167R36 2012
843'.92--dc23

                    2012004233

Partially funded by a grant from the Illinois Arts Council, a state agency

The publication of this work was supported by a grant from Pro Helvetia, Swiss Arts Council

Cet ouvrage a bénéficié du soutien des Programmes d'aide à la publication de l'Institut français/ministère français des affaires étrangères et européennes

This work was supported by the Publications Assistance Programs of the French Institute / French Ministry of Foreign and European Affairs

Ouvrage publié avec le concours du Ministère français chargé de la culture – Centre national du livre

This work has been published, in part, thanks to the French Ministry of Culture – National Book Center

    swiss arts council
                 prohelvetia

www.dalkeyarchive.com

Cover: design and composition by Sarah French
Printed on permanent/durable acid-free paper and bound in the United States of America

WITH THE ANIMALS
NOËLLE REVAZ

Translated by W. Donald Wilson

Dalkey Archive Press
Champaign • Dublin • London

Translator's Note

Paul, the narrator and principal protagonist of *With the Animals*, is an unusual character: a barely literate farmer who lives in almost complete isolation in a remote location, never precisely specified. He has a wife whom he treats with callous brutality: their relationship is summed up by the name he gives her: "Vulva." (The author has confessed that in using this word she felt a sense of shame she needed to overcome, since it was her point of departure for the entire novel.) Paul also has several children to whom he is so indifferent that he is unsure how many of them there are, or of their names. He seems capable of concern and affection only for his cows: they alone are fully real for him. Revaz has described Paul as "a childlike consciousness who has yet to achieve adulthood: he has both good and bad in him, but he has never learned to recognize feelings and is unable to find a place for them in his life."

All of this is seen through Paul's eyes and related in his voice. Indeed, the substance of Noëlle Revaz's novel is at least as much a voice as a character or a story. Paul is embodied by his language. Not only does it display his lack of literacy, his awkwardness, coarseness, and brutality—one critic has described it as "a slap in the face to fine language"—his struggle to express himself especially reflects his difficulty with emotions and his existential incompetence.

In the original French, Paul lives in no specific place, nor does he use any particular form of speech or dialect: his idiom is an invented one. Of course many of the idiosyncrasies of his French are unavailable in English, such as his mangling of the more complex French negatives, his ease in inventing reflexive forms of verbs, and his placement of adjectives before rather than after nouns (and vice versa). Also unavailable was his constant use of the impersonal pronoun "on," used to create a greater impression of detachment and depersonalization than is allowed by its closest available English equivalent, "you." I was therefore concerned to develop a voice that, while delivering that "slap in the face," would not show any strained attempt to write incorrectly or distort the English language unnaturally, but would flow instead from Paul's character and situation. Lacking any example or conventional usage to follow, Paul would have to improvise his language, resulting in a certain stylistic awkwardness. His word-order would be unconventional, reflecting the spontaneous order of his thoughts (for instance in the placement of adverbs or in stating the topic or subject of sentences first, as in *Georges, he said*). His use of conjunctions would be weak. Object pronouns would sometimes be omitted, and the definite article would sometimes occur where no article is normal in English. He would be uncertain of grammatical categories, confusing nouns, adjectives and verbs. His grasp of verb forms, especially of the verb 'to be' (as in *there is* + plural, or *you/we/they was*), and of pronouns would be unsure (as in *me* for *I* and *them* for *those*). Yet he would not use common dialect forms such as *ain't*, and only occasionally employ double negatives.

However, there would also be another side to Paul's language. In particular, Noëlle Revaz has written that in composing *With the Animals* she allowed herself to be guided by the music of words and the rhythms of sentences at the expense of grammatical rules, and I was mindful of this. As in the original French, Paul would at times be quite creative in his vocabulary, coining a number of (frequently 'portmanteau') words. Now and then, indeed, he demonstrates a considerable gift for language, and even a hint of poetry emerges at times, as if to suggest the potential for a more fully human Paul . . .

WITH THE ANIMALS

1

Before when I go out in the morning I've knocked back a good brimmer already and things fall together like straw. Till then I've a face like night on me and a garlic mouth and I can't stand anyone wants to be coddled like a snot-nosed pup. Head under the tap and already I'm getting the machines out. Vulva, she's still dragging round, she scrubs down in a corner and dries off in the kitchen.

There's feeding to be done. The animals, they're astir long before us, they're no slackers, they wait patient till we've finished our purgings to recruit up their strength, to get back to the grind. There's the feeding and then the milking. Vulva, she'd be good help if just she knew how, but already the milk cans is full when still she's hacking about inside, and I go in and find the coffee cold and the toast going dry. Sometimes I eat nothing she's fixed and I never drink what she's brewed and I spit her cooking back at her.

Vulva's a tough nut, she never turns a hair. It's like the animals: when they've seen what a stick is for they think twice before they misbehave, and that's the way to handle them, giving them to remember and respect the master.

Mornings there's a phenomenal pile of work waiting. You knew that before you went to sleep, you knew already from the evening before, but even if you get the urge to go out and set at it again and get well ahead you still have to lie in bed and sleep, but it drives you crazy figuring there's nothing useful you can do all night but waste time. I can lie long awake in the dark if I think about that pile of work waiting. Vulva, she never thinks. Always she goes to sleep off by herself and grunts the whole night away.

If there'd been no Vulva on the farm things would have gone easy. I'd never have had the cost of a farmhand if Vulva had left the spot for some capable body, I'd never have gotten the machines and I'd never have had the debts nor needed to sell land we had from before Pa. There'd have been no young ones, and young ones make work for you. It's watching all day they're not playing on the harrows, it's making sure they're not hiding in the silos when they're filling, and never go gabbing with the farmhand, seeing it can hurt you to learn Portuguese alongside French. Vulva's brood, she didn't make them on her own, and someone has to be father to them. When I have them I give them what they need, and a good hiding if they get too wild, for if you love you lay on the stick.

Life, that's what it's like, all holes and dents and no sport at all, never a pretty picture, and nights when you see Vulva all slattern settling down into bed and churning stupidness in her craw that's still bloated from supper a shame rises up in you and a great urge to lash out that heaves your arm out of the bed and sets you grabbing things and waving them, and I bawl: "For shit's sake, that's enough!"

The thing is, every night, or near, the lust comes over her and she goes rubbing against my leg, and it works you up though at the same time it disgusts, and it'd put the fear into you, the loud moaning and clinging she does. I drive her across to the far side for her to leave me in peace and sleep nice for me off by herself.

Sometimes at night when I take the notion, when I hear her breathing quiet, I slip between her legs and do the business quick, so she won't come molestering me with her hussy's plagueries.

2

At the very start when he came, the farmhand, I said to Vulva: "He's coming, that farmhand. He's a Portuguese. He doesn't speak the language good. He'll have to be looked after for him to stay and not go stirring up the law on us."

And Vulva she said yes.

"And you're not to go hanging about him nor getting thick. This fellow, he's coming to work, so you're not to go showing any belly, he's not one for the women."

At the same time I grabbed her tight behind to let her catch on how and where to contain the lust. Vulva's like that, it's only with the body she understands. The head, it lags far behind; it's set real light, and sometimes I tell myself even if it was taken clean off she'd still be the same Vulva as long as she was left the rest. Thinking's not for her. She never has ideas, Vulva, it all just comes to her from below, and when I tell her that's what she thinks with she says that's so, and it's the truth. She's never understood a thing, all she's good at is making young ones and the business goes with it, but she can learn fast if it's stamped in the flesh. When she has to obey I train her with the tweezers, and that works straight off, I warrant. Or else it's the big stick, like for the young ones, or worse, the rope or the chisel on the wrists, and then she catches on and says yes.

It's due to that inevitable we've stopped talking and there's no more chat heard in the farmhouse, just the young ones playing outside at their yells. But it's real no problem, for that's how I work, in peace and quiet to reflect and focus on the animals. Vulva, she never says a thing out of her trap, she just goes yes, for she always agrees, or else it's watch out dummy. The words come out of her all soggy wet like sludge, so it stirs the disgust in you, and I never let her open her gob when the powers that be come by to say hi and make sure there's no finagling on the side.

Every day she's there beside me, Vulva, and when all's said I've gotten used, for I never see her and never give her a thought. But sometimes God help me I say to myself: "Vulva's a person too!" and I look at her new like I'd never seen tits on a hussy or a stupid big chin and big fat lumps to knead in fistfuls like dough. What a homely one she is, that Vulva! She's plainer than turkey-hens.

It's strange even so, watching her go sometimes, seeing her in the kitchen or feeding the young ones, there comes almost a hankering after something, almost the urge to say just once: "Sometimes you're a good woman, Vulva!"

But never as far as saying it, for there's visions come warning and showing you the sight of Vulva at nighttime and keeping you on guard, for them hussies they draw the littlest opportunities to themselves and twist them for their own benefit. And so when I look at her, Vulva, I like to let on she can think too. It's true Vulva she has her head, she has her eyes and all that. When you watch her going you never think so at all, you'd think she's asleep, but maybe she's just playing dead and she'll rise up and make a revolution, trap me in the cellar. There's things like that happen.

The days I'm watching her she feels it, Vulva, for she tries to profit, softening me with all her sighs: she fancies I'm wanting to get snug with her, so she botches off the housework. But me, I try to talk, I let on I'm ordering the youngsters about, but at the same time I'm watching, and what do I see? That this Vulva can't talk, that this Vulva she understands nothing, and when you say a few words she can only go yes yes yes, and the lips never budge, so anyone would figure she never sees nor hears a thing, for when she's asked for example: "What do you think about them seeds, Vulva?" she gawps off into space and drops the housework and never answers, with her gob stuck wide. So I tell myself this Vulva here can never think, there's nothing inside her head like I've always known, and I cross over to do her a hurt for she gets on my nerves saying nothing and being more gormless than's possible, so I let loose a clout. I like to do that, for Vulva she never lets a squawk but just goes far off, so at least you're quit of her.

Right, and then after that I'm left with the wee ones on my hands. A wee one's no hardship, it just has to learn to keep its mouth shut and clean off its plate, and when it's all gone you just need to yell: "Outside!" It's hardly out of you before there's never a one in sight.

The wee ones they don't like Vulva neither, they don't care for her one bit. They turn up for mealtimes and they're off again as soon as you try to get some profit out of them. Vulva, she puts them to bed at night and it makes them feel to puke when she tries to give her kisses, for you hear the gagging as soon as she closes the door. The wee ones take after me some, but a bit after Vulva too, and that's what puts you off and leaves you never able to take to them nor put their names on each.

3

The day the farmhand came we got the room ready. I'd asked Vulva to clear out a place close to the house, in the glasshouse where we put tomatoes to grow in spring and lettuce in winter, for the glass walls keep the heat in. Inside we put a sort of a bed and a chair, and Vulva brought real clean blankets and sheets with flowers that smelled from the wash.

"Well that's it," I said to Vulva. "That farmhand he'll be waked up in here good and early as soon as the sun comes. He'll never be able to do his shirking off, for the whole place is on view from outside: if he starts letting on he's sick or wants a smoke we just need to keep an eye out and report him."

Vulva she said yes. So then I told her to pay attention and I took her by the shoulders, for she has to catch on, seeing these things is of real mortal importance: "Listen now, Vulva," I said, "when I'm out at the cows or in the workshop, or at the mowing, or on the tractor, you're not to be chatting with this farmhand."

Vulva she said yes. I know well she's no tattler, but I said it to make certain she wouldn't start gabbing.

"This worker that's coming here, he's a decent foreigner that hasn't a penny to his name back home where he's from, so he's looking to put food in his belly with us and make his family happy and put food in their bowls like I do for you here. There'll be no getting in his way."

Vulva she smiled with her teeth to show she's willing.

"I know you're willing," I said just to soothe, "but I know as well what a pester you are when you want something. You're not to go near him: this farmhand sometimes he gets funny urges," I said to put the fear in her, "he likes to clout women and there's one or two he near killed."

She said yes, but I don't know if she thought it, for she's murky in the eyes.

It came time for the mail bus to set down the farmhand. Through the kitchen windows we watched him coming: a great hulk of a worker that filled the whole path, the way under the trees, and the whole stoop and came pounding on the kitchen door: boom boom boom! From close it made you jump, but I wasn't scared like Vulva that ran into the bedroom. So it's the same old story, and it's me left to open the door.

What a strapping great lump, a whole pile wider, a whole pile taller than me! Close up I could see no eyes at all so I had to step back, he was so dusky with dark patches all over where you couldn't make out a thing. I stuck out a hand to greet and he said hi in a funny deep voice. Vulva came back behind and I waved her off, for we had to discuss. The big farmhand took a chair, he sat down at the little table, gave a squy about him, and asked was she my wife?

"Well yes," I said. "That's my wife Vulva."

I thought again about the lines I'd gotten ready about keeping his distance off other men's women and especial the boss's Vulva, for the boss he holds the farmhand's fate and life in his hands, and I started off but the words came out about how obliging Vulva always is but she's useless at working and thinks of nothing but sleep. The farmhand asked where she'd be sleeping, this Vulvia.

"There," I pointed, first giving him the whole tour of the house that's all corners and passages where we store the old wood and the old iron rusting away. There she was in the bedroom, Vulva, stretched out on her belly mending the shirts that's always destroyed after the day's work.

"Out of here Vulva," I said, just as the farmhand he was saying: "Good day, Madame," in his Portuguese accent, and it seemed real strange to hear Vulva called Madame.

Vulva she got up. If you didn't know her you'd have thought she was angry, for she was all red in the mug and heaving her chin up like she was setting to take a bite out of it. But I know my Vulva, and I know who she owes yielding and fear to; she'd be total unable to invent a crabbed face just to inflict me humiliation in front of the big farmhand. I gave her a slap on the backside and said "Out of here!" She never turned a hair and we watched her go, and the farmhand he looked pleased, real relieved to see her big parts heading off, and I said to myself that one is no lover of the ladies either.

Pa, he died in the downstairs bedroom. That's why I told the farmhand we can't have him sleeping in that bed due to the remembrance and faith for the ancestors that we owe no disturbance nor loud talk but reverence and sanctuary. The farmhand he never looked surprised, he seemed to know what a dead person means and a room kept intact out of religion.

"So what are you, Catholic?"

The farmhand went "yes," and "no," with his hands, then he said anyway it made no difference to us, for there'd never be time to get to mass, and personal anyway he's not sure the good Lord exists. It'll go smooth then: seeing we're sending no one to church we'll clear up the farm work together, for there's always work, even on Sundays, and sometimes just as hard, due to the animals that's never done eating.

It's a grand thing, a farmhand.

When we'd looked over the machines—and that takes time, the knobs need demonstrating and the proper connections explaining—and come out in the yard, we went to inspect the glasshouse.

"Here you is Georges," I said, "this is for you, these is your lodgings!" I said like that to make light at the bed and because his name's Jorge, but I call him Georges, for we're no foreigners around here, and bit by bit I was calling him Georges: in these parts the boss calls their first names to everyone, for even they're bigger than him they've got to know all the same who gives the orders. Maybe at first, out of surprise, I called him "Monsieur," or just "you," not out of any intimidation or due to his being so big, but early on I'd rather, for there's got to be concession and politeness, and it's only later he can be called by his name, once there's proper acquaintance.

Georges he felt the bed. Beneath it's no bed at all, just the old wooden gate Vulva set under the sheets and the foam mattress.

"I think that'll do grand," I said.

"Where's the WC?" asked Georges.

"It's out into the yard and then upstairs, but for you that's too complicated," I explained to this good Georges that's not such a giant after all. "You can just go over there . . ."

There's plenty of alfalfa and corn waiting for nothing better.

"Right," said the farmhand, and that he'd like a rest, but I pointed out: "You've seen the time?" and he looked at the time and he saw like me that oh dear! he'd made a mistake, it was nowhere near time for a rest but time for the cows and after that the redding up, enough for three good hours yet. The farmhand, it's due to the journey he was thrown off; it never even crossed him there was cows still to be milked and redding up to be done, so he gave a laugh and said: "I'm coming direct."

He took out some nice blue overalls, brand new and still creased from the folding in his suitcase. I stayed to watch, and I could see his dark legs was like mine, skinny.

4

Now the farmhand's settled into the glasshouse Vulva doesn't want to go in there on her own to fetch vegetables. Georges puts a fright into her, so it's me has to go. Not only I'm risen first in the morning, not only I have to feed the animals, not only work the tractor and do all the field work and manuring, on top of it all I have to come back in when there's nothing to eat, and I figure that's not normal nor legitimate. When the day comes she never wants to rise from her bed at all there'll be just me left to fetch what's needed of food and drink.

I can feel for sure something has to be done, like going over the exercise again: Vulva sometimes she forgets the right way to behave and make herself useful so you have to exercise her when she falls to bits and neglects her duty. It's time you've got to sacrifice and there's things more urgent waiting, but I fork the dung easier if I know Vulva's ready in the house to take the reins and go on her own into the glasshouse to fetch the tomatoes and never look nor tremble if Georges is inside. Anyway, what would he be doing there, for isn't he supposed to be working all day?

With Vulva we did a few exercises for the spiders: when I got her first Vulva she'd scream blue murder if she touched a spider. And God knows there's plenty in the farmhouse. There's great big ones crawls all over the walls, when the light's out you'd think they was rats, and they scare the cows even, wicked skinny yellow ones too that prick the skin and scratch, and they say the spider lays its eggs there. Late evenings in the kitchen and the bedroom you can see how they skate over the whole wall till you can't see the white no more. They must come out of the woodwork nights when it's quiet and look for food in the cupboards.

One evening, why I don't know, I took the urgent notion to break her in on them, Vulva. In the dark I took her hand and laid it to the wall, and she never felt a thing, for she asked: "What are you doing?"

"Feel anything?" I went.

Vulva, back then she was still expressing herself good: "What is it?" she asked, so I turned on the electric.

What a drama! She turned herself all pale, but I grabbed her hand tight and let the critters go to and fro a while.

"You see, Vulva," I said out of sympathy, gentle and not harsh at all, for all the same I could feel she was real shook: "They won't hurt a hair on you as long as you hold still and never move a finger."

But Vulva she couldn't help shifting and fidgeting, and I could see she was stirring up the spiders.

"Keep still I tell you," I was starting to lose patience, "or you'll soon find out they bite."

Vulva she opened her gob, but the sleep of late night lay heavy on her and the voice went thick in her, all clogged up inside.

A green one came with legs you could almost see through, with yellow threads, and maybe carrying an egg. Then I thought that gave a grand exercise to rid Vulva of her fool notions in one shot: if she has no fear of the green one with its egg she won't be scared either of the little brown ones that of course don't sting so bad.

"Come here," I said soft, reaching out Vulva's hand with her going No, but with no real conviction, coming round to the benefit of the exercise.

The green one it came up sudden fast and went into fighting stance with its long legs stretched out frontways like it was getting set to attack. It had smelled the dodge. In the wee second I felt the scare there came a dither, Vulva she made a wrong move and touched the green one and it leapt right on her, full at the nose on her face. She let out such a screech I had to give a slap. The egg couldn't take the shock, and then came the accident: the baby spiders flew over Vulva like darts, all tiny and delicate across the bedspread. The cloth turned brown of a sudden, and I had great sport crushing them by fistfuls on the floor while Vulva she spurted out, rubbing all over with her hands.

5

The other time I picked something easy for the exercise so as not to always make her fail: all she has to do is make the round trip when Georges is in the glasshouse and go past him. It's best to say nothing ahead in case she'd come over with that female timidness that destroys women's self-control.

In the evening I call out kindly, with the soft honey voice I use when there's a chicken needs killing, and Vulva she comes trusting and stupid like I was setting to scatter grain, and she waits with a blank spread over her face.

Hussies like that, they do everything you ask with never a speck of independence to say just once: "It's me getting the asparagus," or: "This evening it'll be polenta again."

They just wait there like a soggy cowpat and spend their whole time rubbing at their faces and asking when we're going to fire up the heating. They never even have the guts to stick up for an idea if they're pushed to decide on their own. Instinctive they pick some god-awful hooey and the worst of pap, and when you're not agreed they daren't even stick to it and they say you're right in place of what we'd rather, which is roar and yell and answer back so we can chat to them with no need to hold back or act coy. But Vulva she doesn't know how, she never takes on to say a yes or a no, and if you made her choose between carrots or cabbage she'd just stand there gawping the next ten years. But I've always appealed to her to speak loud and clear what she has between, and if I yell it's because I want to say too what's in my head, me that's the boss and farmer and master of his house and offspring.

"This evening we'll have tomatoes," I command in a commanderly voice. But then Vulva she gives a leap like the startle of a silly goose that's scared of a shadow, but I get in first and before she begins to bring out any of the slather she's trying to fetch up from her craw I know where she's going and I imitate her stupid dummy's whingeing back at her: "I'm scared of the glasshouse," I go, squirming my shoulders just like she does and doing such a good job that she stops, Vulva, and gawps at me uncomprehensive and I hope ashamed.

"But you haven't caught on, you silly boob, that if I'm sending you it's because Georges isn't inside, for he's off somewhere else. So get a move on, you goose!"

And at the same time I give her a shove with the bowl, taking a good feel at the round humps of her two buttocks that I'd really like to get my hand into today.

Vulva she goes up in front of the glasshouse, but she still doesn't make bold enough to go in, though I'm watching from far and shouting encouragements: "For God's sake, you big floozy, will you go in or won't you? I tell you Georges is off at the fencing on the far side. Holy shit, Vulva, go on!"

But that was a lie, for on purpose I told Georges all considerate to take a nap in his glasshouse and never worry about the work left undone, but to be sure to put his pajamas on, though it's hot, for he's not used to wearing any in bed, as he shows off every night displaying himself through the glass. Georges, he was never expecting talk of a nap. He said, looking up at the sky: "It's not time for bed yet!"

But I talked about the time lag and getting climatized, and that a good farmhand to be rewarded proper deserves good wages, decent wages in sleep. I said for a warning—for you never know ahead how a big Portuguese will react out of surprise: "Don't take fright if maybe someone comes to pay a wee visit," I said with a jokey voice and a wink, and my hands making Vulva's shape on my chest, lumpy in front, and lumpy behind, and her stupid big chin and her toes spread in, but saying nothing more, just enough for him to smell a rat in the grass, and when he spotted her the light would go on and he'd say: "Good God, that's what he was winking for, the boss!" and considerate he'd let Vulva get on with the picking and never scare her with curses or bad words. For sure I can imagine how he'd find disturbing to be roused out of his sleep by some slattern, so I preferred to warn, like a good respectful boss should. Georges he looked like he guessed, and indeed almost right off: "A wee visit?" he laughed, "Well, I won't say no . . ." and he gave his big white-tooth laugh you're well used to by now but the young ones is still scared of. I went on, for I didn't want no upset: "Don't worry if you hear her. If she screams, it's nothing but wind out of her trap . . ." and I gave the wink again, and again Georges he said looking at me: "Oh yeah, nothing but wind . . ." and you could see he'd caught on real smart, and he went straight off to the glasshouse to get ready for the challenge exercise on that big lump of a Vulva.

Right, but now I'm starting to get riled, for this Vulva she won't go into the glasshouse, so what's she up to? She turns round and when she sees I'm off over here but I've the shovel in my hands, then she goes in, and she makes the door shiver, and she bends over and starts picking. There's never a sound to be heard, so for sure the dummy hasn't seen Georges is inside, for she's all calm filling the big bowl with tomatoes and I'm left wondering what's going on. And then there's a move out of Georges, but she stays, so the scheme is working, it's as easy as that.

So then at last it's time to spit on the hands and get back to the slog: time wasted on the likes of her is good hours for getting things done you'll never see back again.

6

When she wants something, Vulva, you can feel it right off: she comes hanging around the cow barn even when there's nothing to do—that is, nothing for her to do, for there's always a pile of chores for us, and Georges he never slacks off, I make sure of that.

The thing is, Vulva she's broken to him now, for the trap worked so good it lasted a whole hour. The tomatoes wasn't ripe yet so she picked almost none, though she went over thorough to make sure. The bowl came back empty plus two or three or five red ones and the half-grown one we threw to the sow. I asked what he thought about it, Georges.

"The trap worked great, she must have been real scared?"

I wanted detail, for him to tell: "What did she do, did she bawl?"

"Oh, bawl, no. Me, I took real care, for the boss gives orders and I always do the job the boss decides."

There's nothing to be gotten out of him, this Georges he's no use at explaining and you can never know what he's thinking. He's a real brute for work and shining up the machines. If he was fit for chatting we'd spend evenings debating and drinking the plum, but there's not a thing to be gotten out of him: when eating's done it's goodnight goodnight and he shuts himself up in the glasshouse and keeps there reflecting thoughts on his own till he puts the light out and goes to bed bare naked.

Vulva, I don't like it, the way she comes hanging about to ask things, I reckon it's not her place. First of all, there's nothing she needs to ask, Vulva, she just has to keep quiet and come when she's called. I can't be disturbed for damn all, for there's a farm to run and it'd take more than a wee Vulva to replace me if I decided to take a break. And then it's one thing on top of another about poor little Vulva, the whingeing of a useless boob that can never make up her mind for herself. Me, if someone comes disturbing me when I'm reflecting and working just to ask if I want boiled or fried, it starts the eyes out of my head and I come over yelling that next time I'll land a clout. And if I've a tool in my hand and I let fly with it, it's a real consolation.

This time she comes up outside, running quick to the cowhouse. When she's looking for us you know right off from the way she has her mouth open and her arms reached out in front like she's running from a gas explosion, for else there's no risk of meeting her in places it's backbreaking and there's no smell of roses: for she has a powerful strong nose, Vulva, and she uses it, and she never forgets to let you know there's a stink.

Well of course there's a stink. Me, a farm that didn't stink, I wouldn't want it. It's just normal a farm stinks, and the farmer that

23

goes with it too, and for the flies to make life a misery for the folk that live on it. Vulva she gets all worked up at the flies, she can't stand to see the specks they leave so she swats them and the butter gets spoiled and she smashes the cheese. She can't shut out things that only bother you if you pay attention, me more than anyone, but that become nothing and invisible if you just stop chasing and harassing them, and can even be a comfort when there's good sport watching or catching them. But Vulva can't do that. She always has a fly circling and annoying her and she gets it worked up instead of leaving it in peace. The fly feels it and gets its sport upsetting her till Vulva gets riled and brings out the swatters and she stirs up the whole host of them.

Vulva when she makes us a visit she never reckons we can hear her coming or that we can hide first so she can't find us. She never even thinks of taking a squy through the window to see if there's someone inside. It'd be dead easy to fool her and get away out the back, but it's no sport making a fool of someone that's hen-brained like her and never spots a dodge and never catches on and never sees how much less smart she is. So I do nothing but just keep mum and never budge a hair when she calls out where are you: it's not right to take advantage of weaker than yourself. You can shout a warning and scold to teach where the limits is and past what boundaries there's a right to chastise and hand out a good clout to print it in the flesh, and that's a rule I respect, whether it's with Vulva—though it's called for a big effort from me, but seeing I'm superior I've no right to harm—or with the young ones that let on they never understand when you yell after them. What you've got to keep in mind is never to be mean to one that could never understand such a level of meanness: for example with the animals it's no use yelling, being as they never understand a word you say. You just have to land them a kick or two and they quiet down, and it's the same with Vulva: I talk in expressions and warnings she's able to figure out, or else it'd be cruelty and mental torturation. And Georges says cruelty's a thing you have to avoid, for it rebounds on you if the victims get aggressive back.

With Georges it's different: when I talk to him I never feel like the master, I never talk like a boss but a neighbor or an equal, seeing he's smart enough and never needs to be scared into working. He explained that clear. In the end I've no need to say another word, Georges and me we work away the two of us like we're one in our minds, and as soon as we catch on we're looking at one another it's time for a beer.

7

She comes in, Vulva. She never sees me for all the dust and the cows going moo and shifting in the straw.

All them cows, I know them and I have their names by heart. I can tell when they was born, what diseases they've had, and their mother's name. I've always had good memory, and from far off I can remember events Vulva hasn't a clue of, she's so hen-brained. That's a game I like to play a lot, asking Vulva if she remembers what happened some day or other and showing she's ignorant, total fogged, like for example: "Say, Vulva, do you remember that time one of the youngsters fell in the pond?"

And Vulva she put on her look of a ninny that can't remember a thing from the day before.

"And when you put on the lipstick?"

Now Vulva, that's total outside her mental range.

"And the day Precious had her calf, don't you remember?" But Vulva she never remembers a thing.

"It was in 1989, a Sunday, me, I remember like it was yesterday."

And when I talk like that precise she gawps back at me dumbstruck, for not only I'm head and shoulders above her physical-wise but mental-wise as well, and in men and in women too, Georges says, that's the main thing, for we're higher than the animals.

The cows, she's never been capable to set about knowing them, Vulva. At first she'd say the names, but she got muddled all the time and she'd call Blossom Brownie and Jasmine Louise. The cows they soon had enough, they got upset and took an offense against Vulva: when she goes past they chase after her roaring, and Vulva she takes fright. But instead if she just took up a big stick that was lying about and did some scaring herself, giving them a good rap on the tits the way the young ones know to do already from they're born, she'd never be fearful again once she saw how they'd turn tail full speed like scared cats, that they's just big sacks you stuff with hay and grass for making into cream.

Georges, he gets on famous with the cows, he has a trick: he talks a bit and they come rubbing themselves against him all friendly and licking in his palm, even when there's no salt. It galls you the way he can win them. They just need a whistle from him to come looking near happy you'd say, though when I call they never even lift an ear.

But me, I couldn't give a rat's fart. There's not a speck of jealousy in me. I'm not going to lose no sleep over it, for it's just incredible Georges he could usurp an affection so easy that's been so many years in the making on this farm. They know who's the master all right and who's the big Portuguese, and they know right well who they owe for the roof over their heads and the dry hay. Novelty can turn their heads for sure when they see some big brawny sort whistling at them, and they run across, for they're stupid, but if they thought a minute they'd see who has the brains and who's the boss and the grief they're causing him, but then they're all females, the lot of them. Sometimes for sure I want to stop them being made fools of. But when I reflect I ask myself what's the use of fretting, for in no time Georges will be off again and the cows will forget and come back to the master looking for their bit of affection.

Georges one time he set out to teach Vulva the cows. Me, I almost had to laugh when one evening he came into the kitchen after the young ones was in bed and I was taking a glass of the plum and Vulva she was sweeping up. He sat down and he said: "Tomorrow I'm teaching Vulvia the cows."

It's strange what he calls her, Vulva. He says "Vulvia" and you ask yourself who in God's name he's talking about, and at first you fancy he's gabbing Portuguese for he pronounces in a funny voice. At the start I tried to stop him saying her name: in my opinion it's not polite to use her first name to the boss's wife. But Georges he would say "Madame Vulvia," and Vulva she made a sign she's no Madame, she's just Vulva. Then Georges he said over and over: "Vulvia . . . Vulvia . . ." and Vulva she said it sounded pretty.

It's odd too to hear Vulva talking all unexpected, it's a strange sound you was never familiar with. It's like a door that's never touched and then it's opened sudden and makes the creak that's been long forgot. Vulva she has a voice would sicken you, all screechy: it mounts up in funny spikes, and if she said the Lord's prayer it'd still sound like she was talking crud. It's a voice would scour the ears off you.

8

I know why she's looking for me, Vulva. There's no call for second sight: for months now she's been pestering me over the pelvis business. She says she has a big ball in her belly, but that's not true: it's just she stuffs herself like for twenty: God knows what she costs in potatoes, but there's no fooling me: when a person eats that much it's no way they can be sick.

Nights Vulva she's always wanting me to feel the ball, to show me the size of it. Well yes, it's true, there's a ball.

"But it's just a bag full of lard," I say. "Eat less and you'll soon find it shrinks."

And it's not even the stomach, it's a lot lower down near the bottom belly, so I figure she's doing on purpose to get me to set my hand there. It's like in the place that swells up when Vulva's expecting and you're left wondering where there's room for the baby unless it's in the barn. Maybe it's some dirty female thing with the innards gone off track or grown outsize due to Vulva being such a gorger and waster of good potatoes. So I say: "Look now, Vulva, we have to put you on a diet," and it brings tears to my eyes I can be gentle like that and speak soft to her, seeing God knows she's mine and I wouldn't want her to be sick or need the doctor.

I said that on purpose for Vulva, to test her resistance, and seeing I know diet's a sure cure for sickness. When the doctor comes to see the youngsters down with a big fever that's what he always repeats: "Diet and bed-rest," and it's always the white lozenges he gives, the ones for the tongue. In the end you begin to figure out it's nothing magical, and as far as I'm concerned before there's any packing her off to the doctor she'd have to be sick for sure and bleeding from the ears before I'd waste time coddling a tender plant like her.

To listen to Vulva it's every day there's something off track with her: Madame gets a pain in the temples when the power saw's running. Oh, does it hurt? So who's the one to use it, the power saw, and who can hardly hear himself when we're doing repairs or fixing up the fences? So I reel out the cable close to the kitchen to make sure she gets her dose. Madame Vulva she feels her pressure low and her heart flittering in the night, she has one migraine on top of another: all of a sudden you hear her loud when she's bringing out her complaints. The subjects that would never tempt her would be to chat a bit about the farm, or take an interest in the master, or talk about the cows for once: that would blister the lips off her. But it's no use crying wolf, I warn her straight, so she should take care not to keep on about it, for normal if there's too much pain I call for the knacker's truck.

Georges he says my legs need attending to as well, for they're all blotchy red and devoured with the eczema. He said it's important to take care of your health, or else people grow old premature and end up in hospital so weak in their lower parts they can't make hay no more nor do their job with the women.

I've noticed how good he is at hiding his cards, Georges: at the start all tight-mouthed with big muscly arms and bulgy shoulders like someone's never had an idea beyond the tip of his nose so at first you said to yourself: "That one, you can shape like butter what's in his head," and you never took him serious and thought you'd be able to pull the wool over him and work him hard and lead him by the nose like the halfwit he looks, but once you're with him a while you notice on account of the language he's sly enough and has his ideas too, and inside that big skull of his he's no dummy and smarter than you thought.

He's well up for example on psychic and mental stuff and about what you should do to women or not.

For example he says: "You see, Paul" (after a bit he said "Paul" to me and though I don't like it much I tolerate, for he's a decent worker and it doesn't mean I've lost my superiority or that I've no authority any more, it just means we work confident together and with equal footing), "You see, Paul," he says, "you have to speak soft, else they're like dogs treated cruel and they bite back."

That gave me a laugh, for I've never found any woman yet could get to bite me, even if I've never viewed any up as close as that stupid lump of a Vulva.

"You understand, Paul, I'm talking to you in images here?" he says to me, Georges. Of course I understand, and I know how to talk in images too: "All them hussies," I say, "I'd love to put a rope round their necks and strangle them like chickens."

Georges he's upset I act doing it with my hands and he doesn't like what I said, so to let him see it's his boss talking that can say whatever he damn well wants about whatever he likes, I add in: "Me, them hussies, if ever I can, I'll make a fire of sticks and burn them up on it. Filthy bitches!"

Georges he never says anything, but you can see he's put out; maybe he's thinking of his own? So I say: "Except yours, Georges, except yours!"

"Me, I've no woman," says Georges, with his eyes all shrunk down into the sockets.

No woman, Georges! Even a big solid-built sort like him, there's none chasing after him away down below in Portugal and he lives in peace and quiet all alone, with no annoyances! He's a real good sort, this Georges: not the kind to go looking for troubles and that's why we get on in spite of him always wanting to chat about Vulva.

"So what about Vulvia," says Georges every now and then, "what do you think should be done for the belly?"

"For the belly, Georges?" I say, letting on I'm in the dark, for Vulva's belly's no business of his.

"We're going to tell them in the hospital?" Georges he goes on.

It's another special thing between Georges and me, and between Georges and Vulva too: Georges when he has a thing to say about Vulva he never says "I," but always "we," and he talks about her like he'd co-signed the ownership papers. Usually that's not a thing I tolerate, for Vulva belongs to me and no one else. Of course there's times you can advise about behavior and the amount of latitude, but I'll never accept anyone telling out loud what I'm intending to do unspoken, that's what I tell Georges, but he explains it's for the best, it's for Vulva's good and mine, and consequent for the good of the farm and the young ones, and if he talks like that it's due to his likes, for he likes Vulva, he likes me, he likes the farm, and the young ones, and even the hens, the cats, the cows and the tractor and the big sow and this whole country, for God's sake.

Well, that starts the tears streaming all right when Georges goes expressing like that. He's sly with his words, for he knows how to talk and he twists them, so it's hard to tell if it's really all lies, except it seems nice and frank and felt true in the soul.

"Good old Georges," I slap him on the back and I sidetrack the discussion to instruct how you can be smart in the head and private at the same time, not like Vulva, and that you can feel uncomfortable at any more talk of showing off a bare belly.

9

Georges, one thing intrigues him every time we're eating is how I came by Vulva. Trouble is, that's a private matter between husband and wife, the way they happen to get married after going together and seeing one another. It's not frequent I gab, it's never, but between menfolk on our own off from the house and eating our lunch under the midday sun with our backs up to the fence maybe there's no risk telling a foreigner how you got caught, seeing there's no Vulva around to hear, and Georges says it only does good to unload and confide instead of bottling all the poison inside you.

Georges, he soon sniffed out that life with Vulva's not all roses but more like a poison that blackens and blights, he says. He has an instinct and a nose: me and Vulva we're not ideal as husband and wife, he says, Georges, being as there's like a lack of talk and conversation. And that means I never chat enough to Vulva nor Vulva to me neither, and that's what the vexations comes from, when for me to talk to her is all that's needed for Vulva to turn nice, put off her stupid mug, and stop being difficult, and she'll say "Good morning Honey" with little pecks and such sweet-talk, and we'll be in love, Georges he explains, like it was in the early days, and it'll be a new life.

"Well, that's okay with me," I tell Georges, "but it won't do for her to come carrying on like that when I'm working in the cow barn, for I've enough to handle already."

It's true, if Vulva obeys it'll get the farm running better.

"But for that," Georges says, "you have to know what the matter is."

That fires up the distrust in me: I've got into my head Georges figures he knows better than me how to handle Vulva and figures he knows her better than me when I've got years of marriage on the clock. I say I know what the matter is, for if she'd just put her back into her duty with no slacking we'd be happier as a couple. For the problem with Vulva is the work, and if she did it there'd be no bar to her earning her man's satisfaction, it's that easy. It's what I tell Georges to show that me too I know how to handle relationships and mental things and I'm ready to forgive as long as she does the right thing on her side.

Georges he seems put out at finding there's nothing he can tell me. He interrogates to know how there came to be love between me and Vulva, and when we met. Well how we met I can't tell, it was one time she came as a poor worker and I got my hand into her like with a wife, for I've my needs too, but just a couple of times, but that's something Georges has no need to know: it's not a thing a master descends to but he keeps to himself even if it's not healthy. So I just tell how it happened that Vulva came with some students looking to pick for the October harvest and she spotted me through the window and saw I was a good-looking sort and took the notion to come and sleep in the house, and I said: "Yes, but only in marriage," and I stop there because there should be no displaying that kind of bodily urgings.

"But at the start," he digs, Georges, "there was love, wasn't there?"

"Well of course there was love!"

There was the wedding, and Vulva didn't want any, but she had one in the oven, so I said it was obligatory to marry if she didn't want to feed and rear on her own, and how would she manage with no man nor money set aside? And that's how Vulva's mine, even if it's a thing to regret.

Georges, I pick up easy, he's the sort that tells themselves: that one there with his pitchfork and his big mucky boots (and maybe with his big thick red neck too) has no feelings, doesn't know how to feel love and sigh and feel his hands sweaty and all his blood hot with passion. He figures I don't know how it is when it comes over you to want the big lump, and you get snug with her, and do what you need for her to stumble, or the way you twist and turn when you go to your bed at night before you've had her yet, just with the need swelling and urging in you. Georges he can't believe maybe I know how or I'm capable even of having a Vulva and holding on to her, for even they're fat, sagging, and shapeless now you can still see it was a grand pair of tits she had on her once, and if Georges is that interested it wouldn't surprise me if he's not so much thinking of me but of getting her into his own bed, and that's why he's always wanting to help Vulva and protect her from the clouts, even if she goes looking for them herself.

That's what I figure out in a blink when Georges asks if there's love, if there's respect and esteem between the parties of the couple. I can show I know all about life between husband and wife, and there's no wee Georges from away that has no woman of his own back home can come instructing me if it's right or wrong for me to be hitting Vulva. So I say: "Way back Vulva she used to have nice pink cheeks and they smelled real fresh."

Georges, he's all ears.

"She never worked hard, but at the start she put herself out more."

Georges, you can pick up he's eager for details. There's the memory of thighs, but that's not a subject for Georges.

"A damn nice filly she was," I go on, demonstrating the round of her hips to show how me I can talk and appreciate about love too and shouldn't be made out a bigger jackass than I am, for if I keep one eye on the hay I keep one on the ladies too.

Though after all that chat about women and Vulva it's no use racking my brains, there's never another thing comes to me except the exercises at the start and the way I shaped Vulva: at the start Vulva she thought life on the farm was like a big holiday, for Vulva she's from the city, Georges he never knew that, and back there she even did things like studying and reading books.

"You'd never think so, for she has a farmy look about her," says Georges, and I say it's education makes the difference, for when we was first united Vulva wore lipstick and she didn't want us to go to bed without brushing our teeth first, and it was me had to teach her from A to Z who's to be master and who the wife, and to complete her education.

And then it's Georges' turn to chat and tell how he lives back there in Portugal, a different country from Spain. Georges he says in Portugal he's no farmhand, he's not even a boss, and he doesn't even live on a farm. Well, that's hard to confide in, for built like he is with them black shoulders of his all bulges Georges is made for the wheelbarrow and toiling in the sun.

"So you work in a factory?" I ask, and pity comes over me when I imagine Georges in the gloom pushing a button.

"No," says Georges, "not in a factory, nor in construction neither."

He says it's not with that he works, holding his hands up like for a joke, but it falls flat. So this Georges is a hell of a mystery, and if women don't want him you have to allow they've good sense. But Georges he explains he works a different way: he works with his head, for even if he's a big strong lad he still goes to school and he's learning a heap of things, though it earns him nothing.

"Of course," I say, and so I ask what kind of work he does with his head, and if it's useful.

Of course it's useful, but it's too hard to explain what for, and why, seeing people know nothing about what he's learning, but if I like he'll teach me: a dead language it's called, and it's a people's language no one talks any more, but years ago it was alive.

"I know that all right," I say to Georges for him not to think I'm ignorant, and I tell how hereabouts they used to talk that way too, and even Pa that's dead and in his grave he used to speak in formulas and I can do the same, and I show him: "Orapronodis," I say, and Georges he gives a laugh and slaps me on the thigh.

We're getting to be great pals, me and Georges.

10

It's not I go in there a lot, to the room where Pa died: I don't like the memories from smells nor the violet bedspread with the photos of the old bugger, but now and again there's a son's duty to be done, like changing the dry flowers or carting off the mice that ate the seeds. That's a duty you have to do yourself.

During Pa's passing over, before he stopped his rattle he had the chance to speak at his last gasp: "Son," he said, "keep up the work after I'm gone."

"Yes, Pa," I answered.

But that wasn't all. "Son," he went again, "look after the farm."

"Yes Pa," I answered.

"Watch . . . out . . . for . . . that . . . woman," he said then.

Then it came like it was repeating on him and squinching up his face. Pa, he couldn't ever remember Vulva's name so he always said "that woman," or "that slut," or "that fat sow," and there was never good feelings between them.

"Watch . . . out . . . for . . . that . . . for . . . that . . ." he said.

"For that what?" said I.

"Huhhh . . . Ooo . . . Vvvvulvvvv . . ." he said and he gave up the ghost that's in God's keeping now up above, unless maybe it's in the place below.

So next morning I ordered up the funeral and they lowered him into the hole, and Pa was never heard of around here no more, except that like he requested in his last wishes his room was kept nice, the way it was the last time he saw the light of day.

I'm not that keen on my side for looking after the dust in his room, for there's always more urgent work on the farm and it's a bit burdensome keeping his place intact and battling the mice and the spiders, never mind all the smut and specks that settle. You wonder where it all comes from: it's a waste of time cleaning, painting and polishing, dusting off the flowers and the iron round the frames, and locking all up with the heavy shiny old key I hide back of the wardrobe from the young ones' paws and spying eyes, for every time you go back in you find the same filthy crud all over the bed and the floor and the mementos, like the room itself was making dust to bring son Paul in for him to look after the deceased on top of all the rest.

I know right well that someone reasonable, a son that'd be maybe less loving and passionate over memory, would tell his woman: "Go in and wash out Pa's room, I've work to do right now," or: "Here's the key to the downstairs bedroom. It's time it was cleaned. It's woman's work."

And his woman she'd go in and take care of it.

But me, I never give up the key and I never let another eye see that room except son Paul's. Already it's enough I let Georges in: Georges one day he says straight out brutal like the ignorant Portuguese he is: "What's in that room downstairs?"

Maybe Georges was out of joint the day I explained, or maybe he still didn't understand the language good.

"It was Pa died in that room," I said, "no one can occupy in there."

Georges, he looked all surprised, and he said: "He's in there, your Pa?"

"Oh no," I gave a big laugh, "Pa's down under the sod, and even the shrews have done their job by now, and he's sucking on the dandelions."

Georges, he doesn't know what a dandelion is.

"So there's no one in that room?" he asked, and he said now he gets why the shutters stay closed: "It's out of respect," he said, "It's out of respect for your father."

And I said that's right, it's to not desecrate Pa, and Georges he said it's normal to honor the memory of one that gave you the roadmap to follow. It's a pity he didn't know Pa, he said another time, for to know the son you have to look at the father too, and he asked was it possible just once to take a squy inside the room, to build himself an idea.

There I have to say I had to weigh the pros and the cons and measure the benefits and risks real careful: on the one hand there's been no cause to complain that this farmhand has spoiled or wrecked anything through his fault, and he does what he's told with no arguing nor foot-dragging. But down in Portugal on the other hand you never know for sure what they can hatch. Then again I've mistrust when someone comes full of sweet talk and civilities: this Georges, he can talk smart and act sly, and he knows to manipulate, like with Vulva when he brought her to the cows.

In the end he happened by one evening when I was taking the key and he saw the hidey-hole back of the wardrobe.

"It's to clean the room?" he asked, and me idiotic I told him it was.

"Come on," Georges he said with that laugh he has when he's set to work and glad to get at it and knows he'll run sweat and it'll be hard slogging, "we'll clean together." It's what he's like, farmhand Georges, thinking of nothing but work, giving pleasure and helping: it lifts his mood and all the time he sings away to himself.

"Well okay then," I said to Georges, "but there's no singing allowed."

I put the key in the lock and I went in ahead and I let Georges in after, and I shut the door behind for Vulva not to come. Inside the room it's dark and you have to know the furniture to tell your way in. Me, I always light the candles to see the dead mice, but Georges he found the light switch that illuminated the whole thing far too bright and showed all up filthy, sad, gray, and faded, with heaps of dead flies on the wood floor.

"Well just look at that," said Georges, "there's need of a cleaning and no mistake," and he started at the flowers, taking out the dry ones; all was left was the paper tulip on the dresser, and he opened the window, for Georges he said they smelt bad, all the old droppings and dirt.

"The room, all this electric destroys its mystery," I pointed out to Georges, "you'd never think there'd been a death in here any more, and maybe Pa would be upset," but Georges he said it was a shame to keep a good room like that closed up, and if you wanted to fix it up it would make a grand place to lodge the farmhands, if any come next year, instead of out in the glasshouse, and he started to plan where to put the wardrobe and the clothes-hooks. It's true it's a lovely spot Pa's keeping for himself. This notion, already from he passed on, as soon as the funeral started, I could feel it nagging: of course it'd be grand to have a nice bright room for sleeping with Vulva, or to put the young ones to bed in, or to keep things in, and there'd be no more need to go cleaning like a female, but there's no farmhand has the power to decide, so it's up to me Paul to resolve it.

"This room, like this it's for Pa and it'll keep for him," I said straight out to Georges to let him know I'm serious and he has nothing to expect. Georges he answered that of course sometimes it's just for sport and it's nice to imagine things, but I'm the master, I'm a free man, and if I'm keeping a lovely vast bedroom like that empty when there's no room to put the farmhand, never counting the young ones still to be born, Georges he can only understand and almost even approve, for down there in Portugal he had an uncle died once, so he knows well the grief it provokes and all that.

"It's not ruled out some day this room will be used," I ended up to console, "but it'll mean it's my turn to decease," I said to scare, and for fear I was bringing down bad luck Georges he crossed himself that no such thing happen to us, not right off anyway.

11

Vulva, she never spots me in the straw, with the bright weather outside and inside the dark blinding her. Let her wait like that till she can see, for at the same time it leaves a chance to take a good squy at this Vulva of yours that you forget to watch all the time you spend with the animals.

Maybe it's true she's not fat, and her chin, when it's all said, you can just overlook, but she's no longer the Vulva of early on with the skirt and the legs lifted up: she's a good decent mother, Georges said, that's had a pile of children and doesn't have nice arms any more, but she's still lovely inside.

Georges he gets on your nerves saying out loud what already you've thought to yourself unspoken, like he was first to know it and yourself you couldn't see you have a Vulva worth looking at and pampering and getting snug with in the night like a husband or a lover. Georges saying she's pretty, that's just too funny and we make jokes, like "lovely hams, pretty hams."

But basical it's more serious, and there's cause to reflect and gather clues for why Georges takes on like that to be interested in Vulva, and if maybe he's figuring the husband's a bit slow? For the husband he sees perfect he has a lovely Vulva for a wife, and this Portugal isn't the first to see it. Second, the husband feels Love for his big lump and he'd not want anyone fornicating her in his place, and they're mistook that thinks he holds the lady in contempt and even has no respect and belittles and hands out beatings: in this heart there's Love and good fresh desire, and I've to hold back not to tumble her right off when she's there handy in front of me in her work apron and her hair piled up.

Vulva she senses like a critter there's someone in the straw, for she calls out: "Is anyone there?" and if Georges figures maybe Vulva has some wit it's seeing he never hears the way the words come out of her like scraps of meat and stir up the urge to give a clout, but Vulva she asks, "Is that you Georges?"

"Yes, it's me, Georges," I go in a voice low down and I breathe gentle in the straw, and Vulva she comes over like one that wants to get snug.

Me then, I kiss her on the neck and mouth like a lover, and I yell "Whore!" and I tumble her in the hay.

Vulva, you'd swear it was the devil rummaging up her skirt. She bawls out, but I put my hand to her.

"Stop the yelling, you Vulva you," I go with a big laugh, "it's no one but your lawful spouse," and I put into her more than she's asking, to let her know all the way who's the husband around here and can give her all he likes and is fit to, and here even if the notion takes him. Vulva she soon stops squirming and groaning, so maybe she's getting the taste for it, but then the urge leaves me.

Georges he's nowhere in the shed, he's not in the workshop. He's not in the glasshouse neither, for if he was I'd have seen, for through it you can make out and see the whole thing if he's hiding.

"Georges!" I shout, "Georges, come here, come here Georges!"

Usual when he's called he comes quick, this farmhand, this son of a bitch Georges that wants to take my Vulva off me and go feeling up her backside like the Portuguese hog he is. First of all it makes you puke, these hog-sty foreigners that haven't even any taste for picking women for themselves or for saying to themselves: "That one's homely, I don't want her." Or: "She has a big chin that one."

They even take on the stupidest ones, ones their husbands have to force themselves to respect and that come rubbing up against them in their beds at night. And then the husbands fancy they can work away in peace, never thinking some prefer women homely like cockroaches and fat as beets and think they're attractive even when they've a split chin and big flabs sticking out. They go all pally to the husband and the husband he tells himself he has a real buddy there and how great it is to have one that never even gives a thought to the hussies, and the trust grows in him.

It's all Vulva's fault, for she's too fat in the backside and thinks of nothing but bed, again in the morning even, and she stirs up the urge to go at it like a brute beast, though she's no beauty: you can feel she's desperate for it.

Georges, now I remember, he went off to do the fencing like I told him, and he's away out of sight in that field over close to the border, away beyond the alfalfa.

Georges, he wipes under his cap when he sees me coming and asks if it's time for lunch already, for the sun doesn't seem high enough yet. So me being the boss, a straight regulatory sort that never beats about a bush, I lay a hand on his shoulder and I ask straight out if it's him Vulva was looking for, and if he's felt any urgings, and if so how come the boss doesn't know?

Georges, he turns red in the eyes and says he wouldn't dare lay a finger on his boss's Vulva and never dreams of such a thing. But how come then he goes singing about how she's pretty and smart if it's not he thinks that's what she's like, pretty and smart and not real fat, and when all's said her chin not too split nor broad?

Georges he catches on what's biting, and he's going to explain the whole thing, and he can swear on the Bible he's never touched a hair on the lady. She's a lovely wife to her husband, the boss that picked her, and she's real kind and nice too. But he swears in his own name, his true name that's Jorge and means Georges, he figures Vulva's too old for him, and anyway it's blondes he has his weakness for, Georges.

"Does that reassure?" he asks me.

Well for sure it reassures, but it still doesn't explain why when I say "It's Georges" Vulva she turns like a lamb and comes across, for if I'm a backward old farmer you'd better reckon I'm a sly fox too.

Now there he has something to explain, Georges, and right now he's not speaking to his boss, his master, his farmer, he's speaking man to man, for hierarchies fall in serious situations: he's going to talk like a male that knows what females is like and the way to satisfy them and make them content, and also how to get rid of them sometimes, but right now that's not what interests us so we'll leave be, and I tell him he can do what he thinks.

So Georges he launches out saying all women need affection. At the start of a marriage you give little pecks, but later you give that up, for us men never like wasting our time and you get tired of it. Do I agree? he asks, Georges. Well it seems I do, about the getting tired at least, for I've no memory of pecks no more.

Never mind Georges he says, the important thing is to be aware the male nature is different than the female. We're a complex affair, we males, but females they're simple, and once you've understood them you can have the whole lot of them in your pocket. Georges he gives a laugh, but not me, and I ask is that the way he gets Vulva into his trousers?

"Wait till I tell you," says Georges. "Women is all the same, they want just one thing off a man: it's for him to give them affection, and that's all they need to be cheerful and happy and content to live and work on the farm, even if their husband is old with a thatch of gray hair on his head, for example, or big mucky boots, or a big pot-belly."

There I've to allow he's right that the husband has no need to be good-looking nor affectionate, for I don't know if women don't care or if they're stupid but they get hitched up with males a whole pile older and more decrepit.

It's easy, Georges explains: when you live with a woman, you have to give affection, just a little taste every day. He's going to take an example to clarify. It reminds him of the cows, Georges: every day what's the first thing I do when I get up to see about them?

"Well, I feed them," I tell Georges.

No, Georges he says, nor actual not just that: he says I talk to the cows and I keep them company, and if one day I say nothing there's less milk the next, for the cows they're lonesome and they've missed the company, and he asks if that's true, and I say he's not wrong, for I remember the way the cows they roar after me if I keep them waiting.

"Well there you are," says Georges, "there's the demonstration you've need of company when you're under custody. Women now, it's just like the cows: they look out for their little drop of affection they need every day. It's a little sacrifice you have to make for your woman to put off her sour looks and set her eyes laughing and her cheeks shining, for her to believe she's happy and get the farmhouse humming."

Well, maybe he's right about this business of company, but that's the husband's job, not the job of a Georges.

"And that's all there's amiss with Vulva, for sure?" I probe him.

"Yes," says Georges, and if maybe one time he let himself get snug with her it's due to holding so dear the farm and the boss that gives him a roof, and he thought maybe it would be doing him a good turn if his Vulva enjoyed a little pleasure.

And Vulva, he just looks at her like a person, like Paul's wife, and not at all like a woman with an ass and tits.

Well then, I say to Georges, that's enough chat about Vulva. But actual, says Georges, it's not her he's talking about, and he's never even thought before of noticing what she's like, Vulva. He doesn't even know if she has legs like this, or a rear end like that, but me I tell him: "Stop!" for I've to reflect on his behavior as a man, and I ask how he knows so much about them if he hasn't one of his own?

Then Georges goes all gray in the face, he says he doesn't know why, why he hasn't the good luck to have a Vulva of his own, a

Portuguese one, to love him and give him young ones. He says maybe it's bad luck or maybe it's due to being a student and close to without a penny, but I say in any case down there in Portugal there's plenty has no money, for they come over here to the farm to shovel muck, and then Georges says maybe he's not good-looking with his big white teeth in his dark face, and I look and say nothing, for it's true his cheeks is like smeared with soot.

He's sitting there in the grass, he's squying down at the ground, and he's down, you can tell, for he's drooping his hands. It's the first time I've seen him that way, Georges, for most times it's always his big shoulders shaking and a big smile wide across his mug.

"What's the matter then," I say gentle like I was talking to Vulva in the early days or this morning in the cow barn, "is it due to the women you're sad? Women's not important," I say soothing, for he's playing deaf and dumb. "They're just bad news and there's more peace without them."

Then I shake him by the scruff and slap him on the backside, and Georges he lets out a few sighs and stands up on his pins.

12

What I've to do now is settle the score with Vulva, hear what she yarns and check it agrees with Georges' lies: maybe I don't look sly or quick in the wit with the mug of someone shifts dung all day and has never read no books so I let on I'm tolerant and I don't mind Georges getting snug with Vulva, but it's not that easy to trap me with honey, and in my opinion, till I get contrary proof, they take their sport when Paul's not around so they're due for their deserts.

It's always the same thing: when you go looking for Vulva she's nowhere to be found, and when you don't want her you're tripping over her.

I shout: "Vulva" all over the yard, but there's no one to answer but them halfwit young ones at their play, doing leaps over the hens and turkeys.

You never see her about the cows no more, so it comes to me I know her hidey-hole: if it's in the bedroom it wouldn't surprise me, for after all the time I've spent with her I know my Vulva, so when she's lying low I can always ferret her out. I shove the door open and there she is stretched out, not a bit undressed, just with her arms over her head and her nose stuck in the mattress.

"I know all's going on," I go to Vulva in my terrible voice, "and there's a punishment on the way to rid you of the appetite."

It's a trap I've set so Vulva figures out I'm wise and for her to cough me up the whole thing and repent in the end.

"If you want to cough up the details, maybe there'll be no slaps," I go to relax her, for I can see no motion in the head or the legs; she's lying there like dead. And when still she never shifts a fright comes over me that maybe she's done herself something stupid, and in place of me punishing her for tempting my Georges she'd sooner be off to the other place below.

"Holy shit . . ." I say to Vulva, and I feel her arm and I'm comforted for it's real boiling hot, and if you put an ear to the dress on her back you can hear the heart skipping along.

"Come on, get up now," I say stricter, "this is no time of day to be lying in bed," and I drag her by the shoulders, but Vulva she won't yield and she covers up her face, so I twist her head round and turn her cheek, and sudden what do I see? That I've my hands all wet and Vulva's blubbering, the pillow is soaking damp, and she's all red in the eyes.

My God, it moves me in the gut to see Vulva pouring tears from the emotion welling up so powerful it starts her bawling. It shatters my soul and sets me shaking deep down, and pictures come to me of the grand joys of the marriage when Vulva was lovely and would still weep tender, so then I say: "Don't cry, my Vulva, it's your wee husband Paul," and I try out a few pecks on the lips like Georges explained that time in the field, but Vulva doesn't allow, so I kiss the nape and under the head, and Vulva lets me, and there comes the urge to be nice with her and get her all snug, but then I remember the hay and the cows that'll start roaring and the machines to be gotten out, but it's just for a moment, for I say to myself I'm giving time to Vulva for her to feel the company and get back her form, and then I pull off my boots and get into the bed, and I tell myself that for once the animals can wait, and I hold her and squeeze her, and I tell myself it's good, for it's sometimes useful, and the work will just have to catch up later, and I get up quick and shut the window and pull the shutter across.

13

And after when I come awake there's no Vulva and already her spot's cold, and just when I take a squy down through the shutter Georges is going by, and he lifts his head and waves a good evening to me, or more like a good night, for the sun's gone, and he says good humored: "We've eaten already, boss," and it comes to me it's past suppertime and I've been lying an age in the bedroom asleep.

Down in the kitchen already the youngsters is gone. Georges, he sits down.

"For the company," he says, and profits to help himself to more bread and bacon, and he goes on about the food and the great soup Vulva simmers up so tasty.

Vulva, she's busy warming up, so she never risks a look behind, and it's just as well, for with the awkwardness rising who knows what might happen if Vulva dares to look round with little scorning eyes? Hussies like her, you can't just let them think they've won because one day you allowed them the favor of getting close and giving an affection better kept for the farm.

Georges he jaws on and on telling a pile of stories and you never know why he's blabbing, except maybe I've a guess it's to offset the silence, for Vulva she has her teeth clenched, and nothing comes to me but pictures from the bedroom. In my head I've the notion maybe Georges believes it's embarrassment, for maybe he reckons he knows what happened with Vulva, maybe he fancies he can guess, but we're setting to show we've no regrets, and if I can talk about it without turning red nor stumbling, like when I'm discussing the cows or normal work, then Georges will catch on that for sure it's not what he thinks and there's nothing to hide.

"Ah, that was a good job back in the bedroom, wasn't it Vulva?" I say to her taking a bite of my meat, and she never makes free to say a thing, but she gives a jump, never daring a yes nor a no.

"We stayed a while in the bedroom there," I remark to Georges, spreading the butter all calm, like I was just saying casual: "I left the barn door open," or: "The hay's not finished yet."

And then right after that I ask: "And how's it with the fencing?" to show Georges if I was talking about the bedroom it was just it came to me one moment and the next it was gone from my head again, for it was nothing important, and it should take none of the thoughts that's fundamental all directed at the farm.

Well, okay, he says, Georges, but actually he'd had something to ask me when I was in the bedroom, he'd had something to tell me that he's forgot right now, and he says he thought right off when he came to the house he'd better not go in, for the door was closed and the shutter across, and for sure he'd done right, Jorge, for later Vulvia said I was lying down and not to disturb me. And then I saw Vulva steal a squy at him, and that gave me like the proof she'd been blabbing to Georges.

But I'm setting to show who's lying and who's telling the truth so for sure it'll be me Georges believes and he'll know the version from that fibber of a Vulva is just yarns too big for anyone to swallow.

"Yeah," I say, after I sent Vulva packing, "I took a siesta of sleep, just a wee half hour, to cure a headache," and Georges goes: "Oh? Oh?" and he asks where it hurt, so I point to my forehead and back over the eyes and I say it caught me a bit around there, but already it's feeling better after the nap.

It's not good to let it hang on, Georges he advises, and he has a pile of medicines about him to treat the cephalalgy. He studied doctoring for fifteen months and he likes to give treatments, though later he realized it suited him better to study a thing more in tune to his character, and you'd never think it, but personal he's a quiet sort that never goes looking for trouble, for even strong like he is with his arms all muscular, he'd rather have peace and quiet for thinking or reading.

"Except on the farm," he adds for reassurance, for he knows very well, he explains, he's here to work, for he's the farmhand here, but off some place in Portugal, if only I could see him, he's a different person, and there's a grand idea indeed, for me to take a trip down there.

"Well, I wouldn't say no," I say, me that has the love of trains and the urge for travel, "but there's the cows to be milked and the yard to be red up, and it's not easy to get away just like that."

Georges wants me to swallow a tablet he always carries in his pocket, but I say it's gone, and the best cure yet, I say, is in this bottle here, and I shove the plum Georges has never touched across the table, for we don't know if he can hold it, and we brim up our glasses and chat on.

Georges he says he guessed what I was up to with Vulva, and it was no cephalalgies kept me in the bedroom. He said that makes him glad and he rejoices greatly and he'd like to congratulate, and I say to talk about something else, but he says he sees Vulva like she's transformed, and I say it's something else happened, not what he fancies, not us going to lie together in bed nor yoking, for there's enough young ones already without further inseminating, but that's between me and Vulva, and Georges says of course of course and he understands that the shutter's for privacy and there's no prying allowed into the spouses of a couple, but anyway he's real glad, and he takes a swig of the plum with a big grin.

So then I say to Georges it's true, he's right, it was no cephalalgies, but it wasn't love neither, and I'm setting to tell straight out what happened in the bedroom. Then Georges he leans forward over his elbows.

"You remember," I remind, "the way Vulva was always complaining of that problem in her belly?"

Georges he says he remembers, and indeed it needs to be looked about.

Well, that's why we closed the door and the shutter, and why we kept saying nothing to him Georges, for Vulva she's embarrassed and wants no one to know about that big ball she has in her belly. She wants to tell him falsehoods, Vulva, but I say to Georges: in her belly the ball's getting bigger, so I had to check, and Vulva she'll explode if it keeps on like that.

We have a good laugh at that, me and Georges the two of us, but then Georges he falls quiet again and waits for the hilarious to pass.

"What's needed," says Georges, "is for the doctor to come."

And in Georges right off there's this notion sprouts: sudden he gets the idea it's him should do the treating, seeing on the farm there's no one but Jorge has knowledge of doctoring.

Then Georges he tries to get up off his chair, he has a bit of trouble rising from the table too, and I stand up with him, not even sure where we're headed, and right then Vulva comes in all unsuspecting saying she's off to bed, but Georges grabs her and tells her to relax and especial not be scared, and we carry her up to the bedroom, her yelling blue murder all the time. Georges he asks me to hold her down for the belly exam. When she hears it's the belly Vulva quiets down a bit, but she's not very happy at me holding her and she starts up her whingeing. Just then in a flood my presence of mind comes back and says to me: "It's your wife's belly that big Georges there wants to squy at," and I forbid touching her, and then there's a minute we're headed for a scrap and we grab one another by the sleeves, but sudden Georges he can't keep his footing and falls flat. Then we discuss, and Georges he keeps blabbing over and over that he understands total what I'm explaining, and he starts up again repeating the same thing and never listening to a word I say and yelling in his other language that I can never understand a word of, so I bawl louder for him to calm down. Then we agree Georges is allowed to feel the belly through the dress, but when we look she's gone off the bed, she's not lying there no more. Georges he runs his hand over the bedspread and says he can feel the ball, and that anyway that's a thing he's never learned about, and he kisses the covers just as I'm lying down on it, and a moment after he's talking about one lovely enough to eat that was nice to him, with great thighs to get a grip of, and the day he starts chatting we'll see what we'll see, Georges he says, and after that he sings a song from Portugal, and in this song it sounds like it's all about Amor, and Georges laughs, he laughs to himself, there's no knowing why, and then the songs turn sad, and Georges is sad and all turned into himself, but I've gotten the best of him and I go off to bed.

14

As soon as the lids lift the eyes blink from the light and I wonder what it is, then I remember I've slept all night with the electric on, and the night before we was knocking back the plum with Georges. Vulva, she's not in the bed, so for once I've room to benefit and stretch out, and I'm just falling asleep or almost when the notion dawns on me sudden that if Vulva isn't here in bed she must be sleeping somewhere else: at half past two at night our Vulva would never be up, not a lazy sluggard like her.

At first my wit tells me: "Let her be, if she'd rather sleep in the passage," and I'm setting to go to sleep again when another notion brings me wide awake, wondering why she's not sleeping here and how anyone could fancy she's sleeping on her own, freezing outside in the dark, unless she's with someone else that's keeping her warm and yoking on her.

So it sits me up in bed when I catch on my Georges is busy with her doing what I did in the bedroom and me here snoring away in the sack like the moron they're hoping.

That farmhand, I've never trusted him. Sometimes now and then, it's true, I say to myself: "He's a good sort," or "He's worth his weight in gold, " or "Well, down there in Portugal there's some that's strong in the arms."

But right off the suspicion rises in me and I see how he strokes and the way he talks about her and how he coaxes the animals and always acts nicer than is human possible when you're doing mucky work, so I say inward: "That one's not straight, better find out what he's hiding," and deep down: "In that soul of his it's not clean," and when I've my eyes open I gather up clues this Georges is a deceiver and thinks different from he chats.

I never said a thing at the way Georges came revolving about the animals to teach them to Vulva. I let a laugh in my throat like some half-wit old dodder easy to fool, and when Georges inquired about her out in the meadow I put on like the tone of a husband that reckoned it was regular to tell all about his wife, and would never see a thing wrong with going to bed in a glasshouse bare naked or getting familiar going "Hi Paul" to his boss, so Georges he got it in his head he could carry on like that, seeing backward old Paul never notices what he's hatching.

And then it comes back to me about that song from the evening before, about his blather before I went to sleep, going on about some lovely female, and it sparks off in me: I see now it's Vulva, for the grand thighs fit, and in a flash I catch on to all that's behind his words: drunk on the plum Georges he showed me his whole hand.

It was by good luck I slept in my clothes and I never lose a second pulling on my boots. I take the stick with me I keep handy for bandits or burglars and to make sure no one comes round looking for trouble. It's a grand stick for basting dirty swine and stinking trash, that's what I tell myself inward, and it does you good to put it in words, even if you can't speak out loud for fear of scaring them off and letting them know you're on your way to give a licking.

It's busy in my mind while I'm going, building up my plan of how to carry out the attack: first I've to get close up to Georges' glasshouse and slip in back of it, seeing beside the alfalfa there's room to walk. Georges busy squeezing and snugging up to Vulva he'll never have time to know his boss is onto him, or maybe even he'll be asleep, wore out from reaming her.

Then when I get there I'll take a squy and study if there's a way to get in and if Vulva's in the raw. It might even be good fun to see her bare-assed once, and turn the light on bright for the ridicule and to show her she's witless and fat as a peach, and maybe even Georges won't want to get snug with her any more, and he'll start laughing with me, and we'll split our sides and pack Vulva back to her place in the kitchen. For basical it's easy to forgive him, Georges, as long as he's ready to see Vulva's just a lump of pudding dough. A fine strong handsome lad like him shouldn't go throwing himself away on the opposite sex fancying it's a worthwhile career getting them into his bed. Maybe there's still time to set him right if we show him Vulva's leading him by the nose with seductive sights of her rear end and all that.

From the yard already you can see the glasshouse all dark: that means either they're asleep after doing the job, or else they're hard at what we did in the bedroom, Vulva and me, and can't turn on the light for they want no one to see, like me for example if I got up for a pee or went looking for Vulva after finding I was sleeping alone, so I tread real soft.

This glasshouse, you can see right through it: on the other side across the rows of tomatoes there's the farmhouse with its shutters closed and its roof solid dark and the sky bright overhead, for autumn's coming on slow and it's not so warm these nights. You can see the bed on the alfalfa side and the litter of papers falling out of the suitcase, and the blanket too, and the sheet shining bright, for there's a ray of moonlight.

But especial you can see there's no one inside, and it's still like ready for bedtime, and if Vulva's not there and no Georges neither there's no call for book-learning to tell they're lying somewhere the two of them together.

"Dirty scum," it comes over me to mutter.

It's then the notion lights up in a flash: Georges he knows the room Pa set aside for himself, and he saw where the key's hid too. I can hear him like it was yesterday saying it's a shame it's not put to better use, and right off the whole story unwinds black on white like I'm seeing Georges inside: why Georges tricked me coming to spy on me taking the key, why he lets on he wants to do the cleaning when already he has the weight of a whole day's work in his legs, and why he was preaching me like a sermon all the time, letting on he was just saying out loud what he thought but never trying to influence nor decide in Paul's place.

Now it packs me all through and roars in my ears it's so disgusting to see with the inward eye the way Georges is making a fool of my Vulva, leading her on a bed of roses and then doing it to her on the violet bedspread that was left in Pa's name and never intended for no Portuguese nor slut of a woman. Let her moan, Vulva, and let Georges go at her, and let them jiggle their backsides and drool, it's a foul thing you'd never want any part of ever again. When he's at the trough the shame will come over Georges and he'll want to give Vulva a clout and tear her to shreds, for she stirs such a powerful loathing in your head you want to puke and clear it out.

But there's never a soul to be found, seeing the key's in its hidey-hole, and when I go up close to the door to hear if there's a sound and peep through the keyhole to see if Vulva's lying there flabby pale, there's nothing inside but the dark and the mice nibbling, and it looks like the door hasn't budged since I did the dusting and took away the dry flowers.

So then the problem is to know where they're lying and solve the puzzle of how Vulva, her sensitive to cold like she is, can sleep outside in the freezing air, even with a man shifting on top of her and covering her against the cold? But I've no time to ponder the question when I hear the mattress shifting in our bedroom and straight off it tells me it's Georges going at Vulva on the marriage bed.

"Oho, less noise up there," I shout up the stairs, and it's too bad if the youngsters cry out and it gives them nightmares.

"Damn me but I've caught you this time," I yell from up close, and I shove open the door that has no light coming through, and in I go big and tall. Vulva looks like she has no notion what's going on, and she's scared stiff for she hides under the bedclothes, and you'd fancy she'd been long asleep for she's dark round the eyes and wearing the flowered pajamas shrunk from the wash. She's not naked at all, for I take a squy under the sheets and she has the bottom on too over her legs all spread out and flabby that you never want to see.

"Where is he, Georges?" I bawl at her: "Georges, where is he?" but it's no use looking, for besides the bed and the chamber pot there's nothing else in the room. Vulva, she makes a mumbling that clogs up her gullet, so I have to bawl three times before the voice comes back in her, and then I find out she doesn't know, though she thinks normal it's in his bed he sleeps, and I get it out of her that Madame was so scared she hid with the cows till I went out into the yard, and she was in terror of us for we was drunk on the plum.

"Drunk?" I say, "Drunk?" and I let loose a clout at her like I've not given a for long time to let her learn if I've the aim of one that's drunk or sober, and then I drive her across to her own side and I lie down in her spot and snore, though I know that's not the end about Georges, and the youngsters is bawling in their beds.

15

It's the little van, the little red and white one that bangs its doors and parks in the yard just when I'm going out front to catch the fine day rising.

"Well here's a surprise," I go to the doctor after he's dragged himself and his bag out of his old crate: "it must be a few months since we've seen you about here," I go on to have the air of someone pleasant that's always in good humor and jovial from early morning and sees no snag to welcoming and offering a cup, and who's maybe glad to see the doctor even he doesn't feel sick nor anyone else on the farm. But it's the very opposite, for since he's joined up to the Board of Health he never comes on us except it's unexpected to check the dung's kept apart and squy at our gums to see if they're dirty.

"What wind blows you in here, Doctor?" I go like a nice sociable sort that has no mistrust nor anything weighty on his conscience, though I can see from last evening the whole yard was left lying open and there's fresh cowpats from yesterday all over the place that maybe he's stepping in.

"Well, Paul, it's for the patient," says the doctor looking surprised, so I ask: "The patient?" and right off I catch on it was Georges that sneaked and called in the doctor, maybe when I was out in the fields or working the tractor.

"Come in then," I go friendly, thinking fast how to fix it that he never gets to squy at the belly.

"You're on your own?" asks the doctor, looking out across the land.

"There's Georges, from Portugal, that helps with the work and the cows and the fencing."

"Oh yes," says the doctor, bending over his cup like he already knows about Georges, and it confirms me I'm caught in their trap.

Anyway, there's no Georges in sight yet, and that's not habitual for him, for mornings when I come out he's waiting like a faithful dog for me to open up and dole out his portion, but last night due to the plum he likely went to sleep outside.

And the patient, the doctor he asks, maybe she'd be ready to let him examine? For he has a lot of patients far from here that has fevers and he has to go driving all over the place right into town. For sure she's up, I tell the doc, but mornings isn't the time of day she hurries most, so breakfast is always late, for Madame Vulva she takes her own time at washing, and then I shout up the stairs: "Vulva, come down!" and she comes straight, for out of the window she'd seen the doctor coming and got dressed quick on purpose for him to think I'm a liar and she's always up at the crack of dawn.

"Good morning," says the doctor, and Vulva goes "Good morning," with a nice shiny face and a lovely smile you'd take for a mask.

"Where can I carry out the examination?" asks the doctor, and Vulva she answers: "In the bedroom," and she's well able to speak out clear and she's put on all her finery like for a party.

We're setting to head up the stairs when Georges turns up all ready dressed in his work clothes and his hair all tidy and no look of having slept anywhere but in his own bed: hearing the vehicle driving in of course he wanted to come and see if it was the doctor and if he can take a look at Vulva. Me, I just let Georges go on, I let him say good morning and do his kowtows and smiling up front, for at first you're in shock and daren't say no nor refuse his request, but I know the doctor keeps the professional secret and he'd never let a big dago of a Portuguese anywhere near a female patient naked about the low belly, and I've no worry on that score, for the other time he came he didn't even let in her lawful husband, and he stayed a whole hour, and I never even knew for sure what was going on.

"Good morning, Georges," says the doctor, and him greeting right off like that and knowing his name straight away without asking when they was never introduced, that struck me real strange.

Next the doctor and Vulva go up into the bedroom together with no stopping them, and the doctor he turns round and asks how long it's been swelling up, and before I can tot them up Georges chips in with the months and tells all the details going in, and then Vulva goes on the bed, but the doctor doesn't make like he's setting to send us out of the room, us males.

"Maybe we should leave?" me I say to the doctor, relative to the propriety, for you shouldn't look, and to remind about the medical secret.

"Well," the doctor looks surprised, "if you want to stay, Paul, you can, if your wife consents," and we all look at Vulva but she never lets on a thing and there's no telling what she thinks.

But I don't give a rat's fart for Vulva, it's Georges I want out, but he shows no sign of budging or any such intention, he just lets on he's not listening, but he carries on chatting to the doctor asking questions with no discretion and total at ease.

"I think I'm going, this is no business for men," I say to give the lead, for Georges is total obliged to follow the husband if he goes out, and I go, but slow to give Georges time to reflect on the hint he's supposed to follow.

Georges he just keeps talking and explaining to the doctor and he never hears I'm going, and me I've the respect not to go shouting in front of the doctor, so I repeat in his ear: "I'm off to take a little walk during the belly examination," and Georges he goes yeah yeah, and takes a squy at the belly but he never budges a fingernail.

"I'm leaving, for I figure it's real dishonorable to go prying at sick folk," I say out loud for all to hear.

The doctor he looks up and he says: "Yes, you go Paul, and maybe you'd close the door after you," while Vulva she's taking down the start of the pantyhose, and I'm forced to go out with no ability to go back now, if the doctor has given the order.

Now that's a thing not possible to tolerate for two males to go poking at my Vulva, and she all consenting and open, here in my own house, under my own roof, and me not there to say "Stop there, that's far enough" at where they're setting to stick their paws.

But I know an easy way to flush him out, Georges. I go under the window and I call: "Georges! Georges! Georges!" for a good long while till Georges he comes out all riled at me through the window and asks what's the matter.

"There's three cows got out through the gate," I say: it's an emergency can't wait, and Georges knows it, for he answers: "I'm coming straight," even if now after keeping company and chatting with him I'm getting to know him and I know for sure he's upset from just seeing his dirty dark head and the unwillingness damping his smile.

"Which way?" he asks, Georges, after he's come out front and he sets off for the meadow with the look of a man put out of his humor.

Meantime I go back up and put my ear to the door and my eye to the keyhole: the examination's done, for Vulva's sitting up straight on the side of the bed with the doctor beside, and they're taking their time to chat.

Vulva, she's acting ladylike, starting to speak clear and making up grand sentences so it sounds like she's twittering, and the doctor he's all charmed, for he almost lets himself go into her hands, but just out of sympathy I reckon, and saying she's not that bad and in the hospital there she'll see how good they treat her.

The hospital?

But Vulva she carries on with the play-acting, digging up vocabulary I've no clue where she gets it, and she even puts on a little false pitiful voice: she yarns that her husband never treats her right and she's had enough on this farm, and she starts up her complaining, but the doctor he goes back to ferreting out about the husband. He wants to know if she's scared of him, and Vulva she starts sniveling, that big lump of a Vulva goes blubbering saying she can't take it no more, that her husband persecutes her and she feels he has no respect.

Well as far as that goes she feels correct, and I'd never have thought she could pick up so well what I have back of me. Me, what gets my goat is this snoop of a doctor sticking his nose in outside the Board of Health: that makes me spill over and I shove the door in yelling: "That's enough bullshit!" and I grab Vulva by the hair: "What lies are you telling the doctor? There's no better husband than me out there. If I'm not good enough for you you're nothing but a boob and no use for anything except turning good men into hogs."

And I head for the doctor but he's almost out through the door: "It's not allowed to go poking into the parties of a couple" I say, as I recall, "and it's nobody's business but mine."

He's caught on all right, the doctor, for he gives a nod, and then after he goes downstairs I hear him telling Georges quick that's back from the fencing: "Till Monday then," and that's when I see clear Georges knows all about the hospital.

16

In the hospital they look after you and then you're cured, it's cram full with nurses and women that's doctors for taking good care of the belly, Georges says, for they've all the equipment and medicines to treat Vulva best, better than away out here on the farm where there's no rays nor chemotherapy.

We've sat ourselves down to take our rest in the sun, out there in the meadow where you can't even hear the young ones no more and it's past time for lunch.

Georges he says we'll have to wait, you have to be patient like when you put sulfate on the fungus in plants. Vulva, it's the same with the fungus in her belly: they'll make an incision in her and then they'll put in a kind of sulfate, and it'll be beneficial for sure.

After that Georges starts acting through the operation, but I get like weaknesses tickling me in the legs and like a veil over the sun, and my feet is taking off, so I tell him to tone down and not gab in so much detail, for my gut's heaving and I'm close to keeling over.

"Okay! Okay!" Georges he says, but he goes back all the same just to finish off. He says he's sorry but he has just one last thing to say. Once the ball is out they take a needle and thread and stitch up the skin to make the belly smooth again. It's a lovely job, says Georges, and it's a shame he's kept back here with the animals, for he'd have liked to watch them medics at their neat work.

Now Vulva's gone we're back on terms, me and Georges. It's not that I wanted, but I was real forced, what with the farmhouse to be looked after on one hand, and the animals on the other, and the fields on another again, and the watering to be done, and on top of that the young ones to be fed and wiped. Then there was the problem of the cooking: her being a woman it was always Vulva made the meals, but after she left we had to make do. It's not I was unwilling to cook stews or soup: on the one hand even I'd rather, for it's light work and not hard to keep up now that already the canning and the fruit is in the pantry, but on the other hand without me the poor old farm goes down the drain: it's only me knows how to keep it running and even Georges still there's things he needs to ask.

So we talked it over thorough and decided he'd fill in as the woman for looking after the housework and washing up and cooking meals as far as possible, and as well lend me a hand between times, and go back evenings to cook supper.

He cooks good, Georges, better even than Vulva herself, though she can compete with the little tarts. Georges he cooks us up new recipes, strange specialities they eat down in Portugal every day of the week. All the time, he explains, Georges, they eat grilled fish, for they're common as grasshoppers down there, there's swarms of them everywhere, and they cost nothing to eat, but here you can't for there's no sea nor ocean, just polluted water where no one catches the trout and there's manure dumped along the river. Since we've no fish Georges he says we'll cook instead the same recipes with pork, and he's right, it's real good, it sets the juices running, though the youngsters never believe it and they won't touch their plates.

Even it's good, me I'm in the dump since Vulva left and just when I fancy the appetite has opened up as soon as I put fork to mouth it clams up again and I feel like a vomit coming: it's psychological Georges he explains, it's all in the head, it's due to me feeling the emptiness of the gap left from Vulva being away, and it makes me mad I can't get down this good dinner that goes to waste and Georges shovels down his craw.

I know well it's not Vulva takes the stomach from me, it's not the little gap she leaves, for it lets you breathe, it makes room for peace and quiet at last not to have her always like a fly at your back and like a big rat in the bed. No, what's bothering me, I say to Georges, is the whole run of shocks: the first was finding out Vulva wasn't faithful and was carrying on evenings with a brown weasel of a Portuguese I won't name, but you know who I mean. To that Georges he says he pleads not guilty again, and I say he has a reprieve, for there's need of him, and anyway I don't hold against him, for what do I care for Vulva, and we should stop right there if we don't want a falling out.

The second shock was when the doctor came, being betrayed all of a sudden when you was trusting. Georges he hangs his head and sidetracks the conversation, but you can real feel in his heart he's reflecting over and upset at himself for destroying the trust of a good pal like Paul.

Me, I've always had a knack for knowing what people is hiding, it's like I've grown antennas or whiskers. I learned off the cows. When I go close to one and sit down and touch her, straight off I pick up what she's ruminating inside: if she has enough hay, if she needs salt, if her nerves is ragged due to the thunder, or if she's getting set for a dunt with her horn and you'd better keep clear.

"Poor old Georges," I go when I catch on he's smarting deep in the spot where he's sad, "I can grant you a pardon, if that's what's tormenting you."

But Georges he acts surprised, he says no, there's nothing of the past needs correcting, for it's over and done; then he eyeballs me straight and says he's guessed who I'm sad after, and he's sad too and he wants to console me so much it hurts, seeing someone suffering close to him: he's had a great idea he's going to propose and if I'll just agree to wait it'll be a surprise, like a gift the farmhand he wants to give, from Jorge to Paul.

Me, a gift, I'm not saying I'd mind one, but I never say I'm agreed, seeing they say there's some can poison you. But it's no matter, Georges he says, all he's asking is for me to trust I'll be pleased afterwards and moved to my gut, maybe even as far as shedding a few tears.

Trust's a thing a person can give, and he can even let on he's giving it, seeing it's transferred invisible, so even he says he's giving it he can still keep it for himself, so I say yes, and Georges he shakes my hand like he was council chairman, for he says he knew ahead I'd accept and say yes: now I just have to wait and sit still till Georges calls me, and if I like there's even time for seconds.

Georges he leaves the kitchen. It's not real hard to guess what he's off to hatch: even deaf as a potato or an old sixty-year-old you can hear him from here moving about and you can tell already he's fixing the surprise over the phone, rounding up some neighbor sorts for the plum.

That phone, it cost a tough battle against the old bugger to get it in, back when he was alive and a detriment to business and the farm. At the start it was me put up the idea we should get the wires put in to keep contact with the vet or order up a farmhand or there's a cow for the bull and so on, and for the doctor and the priest too, who, as unfortunate it soon turned out, was needed urgent for Pa: when he passed on all was needed was a call and inside two hours the priest he was there bringing his purifying water and his prayer formulas, and it was thanks to the phone we was able have Pa taken away and give the order for the burying and get the undertakers to look after the coffin.

That's a thing he should have seen at the last, Pa, for you can't be stuck away all isolated alone like us on the farm when everybody else is chatting together and gabbing to one another over the wires about what they're doing, nor have them laughing at us that we never hear any news and live here like it's still the nineteenth century. You have to move on: us, we've got the electric cow-trainer and the toaster, and we'll have the Walkman when Christmas comes. That's the surprise I'm giving the youngsters: a nice musical Walkman you can listen to all by yourself outside, away out across the land and in the cow barn even, just they'll have to watch out they don't run down the batteries too quick.

Pa he thought he was the only one standing head and shoulders on this earth, with his farm, his dog, his son, and his big lump of a daughter-in-law he can't stand and he says is a plague. That's how he ate away at himself till his heart was ground down and turned sharp and nasty like a wasp. He could never open his eyes nor take an interest in the lovely things there is in the world: me for example I'm a farmer, a countryman, and I've work enough to keep my wit occupied. Even so, sometimes in the day I think of other things that aren't there, invisible things, and I tell myself stories about them and in my head I take a trip off the farm to clear the mind and keep alert mental-wise.

Sometimes for example starting from a beet or a cornstalk I say to myself just like that: "I wonder how much they made last year, the neighbors?"

And then I go over to their place in my head and I work out the area of the farm and how many acres they have. Or else I fancy I need to replace one of the cows and I debate over the breed and the breeder's name, and I take trips all round the world and I lay myself open to everything.

If I'm digging the sod and I come across an earthworm, I start looking and expanding my ideas and taking an interest. Some folk never turn a hair but smash straight down with the flat of the spade, and there's some slice clean through and kill with never a thought, never allowing any notion that critters might have stories too, stories just like ours, only we're bigger. I never cut through an earthworm thoughtless, and with him squirming there what I really like is to tell a story about how he's lost his direction and feels the spade coming down and he's a worm farmhand and he has a worm boss and a squirmy lump of a wife back in the farmhouse, and he's maybe asking himself in this spot where's his field and where's his farm with the animals and the hay. For sure it makes him shudder, the metal coming down from high, and he strangulates himself trying to get away, and he never knows there's a person guessing and seeing all he has inside his head, for you're so high up and so much freer in your thoughts and you despise his squirming. There's no avoiding big peoples' spades: it's a sad day for the farmhand that couldn't escape before and is left no choice but to die the death he's looking for.

That's the way I keep entertained and alert.

But Pa, he never could, he was never smart enough to open his eyes and turn them somewhere else, so he died alone, stupid and bad-tempered all through, and he never learned to work the machines nor talk into the phone.

Georges he comes back from the passage. He looks all excited with his eyeballs shining. He wants the boss to come and talk into the phone. No problem, I inform: from years back Paul's handled the phone with no trouble.

"Yes?" I go clear into the little holes and then I go quiet to let the answer come to my ear.

"Yes?" I go again, but it doesn't seem to be working for the only thing comes is a sniffing. Then Georges says to me private without the phone hearing that it's important to talk agreeable and say this is Paul speaking.

"Yes, this is Paul," I go very agreeable, "and who's that off at the other end?"

And then I have a surprise hearing a little shaky voice, almost crying: "It's Vulvia," whispers Georges, "it's Vulvia speaking from away there," and then I want to say something but it catches me in the throat.

"Vulva, is that Vulva?" I say all quavery before any other words come out, and I can find nothing except just go over and over: "Vulva . . . Vulva . . .," mechanical, like a half-wit that's lost its tongue, so Georges he encourages me and prompts the words at me: "This is a real thrill," Georges whispers low, and: "How I've missed my Vulvia."

But I just jaw on: "Vulva . . . is . . . is that our Vulva away there?"

Georges he makes up going along: "When you come back we'll have a little party with sangria."

But me I'm still mumbling: "Is that . . . our Vulva, the one off our farm?"

"I love you," Georges murmurs and all of a sudden the whole thing fits together so it freezes your blood and your wit and brings you back on earth where there's problems and memories of the times Vulva lived on the farm.

"For God's sake Vulva," I say at last, "what's going on in that hospital?"

Vulva she can't answer too good from blowing her nose, so I take her chatting time to give her news of here with her away: "There's Georges, he cooks fish with pork," I tell her in my nice soft voice, "but you should come back soon to make the little tarts," to pay a flattery and for her to quit her blubbering, and it's only later

I remember she has that hole in her belly and I ask if she's able to eat, and if the stitches on the scars hurt, but Vulva keeps blowing her nose all the time, and Georges says she's getting fatigued. He takes back the control and says quick: "Talk to you soon, good-bye, hugs and kisses from everyone," and I tell myself he's making very free hugging and kissing her on my behalf in front of and beknownst to the whole farm, and then Georges shuts off the phone and I go back to my chair and wipe away the drops still hanging.

17

Georges he reckons if she's crying it's not due to them hurting her there but that she's missing the farm so deep, and the youngsters, and her beloved husband, and maybe he's right, I confirm to Georges, for always she's wanted frequent contact as a wife and her man's affections, though giving no details of the frictions and rejections that fall out from it to me.

Georges is gnawing the bones from the chicken he cooked for dinner and the youngsters ask for seconds, for they know which one they're eating, seeing they played with it before Georges picked it and plucked the feathers.

"You have to gnaw right to the bone," and he shows them how.

He demonstrates how to break it and the marrow you can find inside, and while he's doing it the longing comes over me for before, for when Vulva was around and all you needed was a shout for her to turn up and be ready for orders.

It's not I've feelings for Vulva, it's not she means a thing to me: Vulva's no closer to my heart than any other floozy that might have slept at my place, in my double bed, in my farmhouse, and have carried the young ones that is mine too in her womb that I've always kept well supplied. Anyone would be troubled at a familiar presence missing and wanting. Since she's away she's left things off kilter on the farm due to her absence, for it's like if a screw falls out, even a rotten old rusty one, the machine stops working, and on the farm too there's something missing, even though she's of no importance, so you have to get back your grip and your rhythm.

Georges, whether it's from the newspaper or books, he calls it the "feminine presence," and believe it or not there is such a thing, even with the likes of Vulva seeing I miss the sight of her, just for a moment anyway till it passes off and I get back my hold on myself.

Georges he has a whole theory: he says about women there's something special that fools us, for we're not smart enough to catch on and see it: you can only feel when it happens, and it's the Mystique they write about in books. It's what makes us love women, Georges explains, whatever the shape of their figures or their degree of ugliness. It's not hard to believe, seeing that without some magic or trickery they'd never get us to stick with them permanent and stuff our heads full of them.

Maybe it's true she's homely, Vulva, but in the kitchen it looks nice most of the time with her there. She goes well with the furniture and the oak dresser, so when you come in and she's not sitting there mending a shirt or standing around cleaning, or even when she's not sitting there gawping off into nothing, you just can't get used to it: you feel things is all empty bare and a sadness comes over you, and if you never open the plum it weighs on you again, and the mind starts stewing.

"You've got the blues, Paul," Georges says every time he comes in and finds me at the plum, and he lays an arm over me before he pours himself a glass, for now he's got the taste for swilling a drop himself. And when he's taken some he sings songs in Portuguese, in foreign words he makes up just for me: "It's the lonely husband blues," he announces when he starts off, always to the same kind of tune, and he reckons maybe I like it, but it leaves me disturbed and I like better when he stops and goes off to bed and I'm left reflecting on my own about the future and the farm.

Evenings I count up on the calendar the days we've spent with no Vulva: twenty mornings since the doc came to look at the ball, seventeen the vixen has been off coddling in the hospital, and twenty-one since in full daylight we lay together shameless in the bedroom.

I marked the days with circles for a reminder.

Husband-wise I can't say I feel a frustration. In the flesh there's nothing calling for satisfaction, no tortured obsession, nor in the head neither, for it's healthy and keeps working with no need to give base pleasures from female visions, and down below is serene, glad to be left in peace and in no need of thoughts about going off to visit others.

When we take a cow to the bull, even then I get no pleasure at seeing the maneuvering or laughing at the beasts slip-sliding and struggling with the effort when for sure they'd rather be out grazing in the field. All the while she's being done I prefer to be drinking coffee with the owner of the male that's the future daddy of the calf: not so much that I feel shame or modesty at the whole business, but I get all sweaty in the legs and disgusted and nauseous from the heat when I look at the way the bull goes at it with the lookers-on circling round the female to watch how the husband climbs on her and skewers her, and the way she shifts and roars under him, like it was nothing good he's stuffing up her.

Georges on the other hand he likes coming along to inspect the whole affair, and he runs a commentary for anyone that maybe never witnessed the carry-on.

"Come and see your cow, Paul, come and see the way he's taking her," he calls loud to me, just when I'm forced to answer all of them that's asking: "So how's she doing, the wife?"—even ones you don't know and never want to know.

Since they heard she's on treatment they're chattier than ever: "And is it true she's sick?"

"Now what was her name again, your wife?"

There's always one to say, with eyes sharp as chisels and a wink: "Vulva, that's her name, right?" and I've no time to answer before they all burst out laughing together, but I've no way to tell the whys and wherefores of how she was given that name, Vulva.

I have to say these jokers take advantage of having me in the pinch to try to find out everything they want to know about the farm and me and the family, seeing it's not often I go drinking in the village looking for tittle-tattle or gossip or consorting. They try to drag out a whole pile, but it's Paul the carp they're talking to, it's tight-mouth Paul, that's never so quick to cough up the fly when he doesn't want to.

After the cow's served we go back to the farm, the four of us, myself, she, Georges, and the embryo putting down roots in her belly. If the bull hasn't taken her right we go back a second time to perform the whole circus again: the bull, Georges' commentary, the café and the lookers-on, and the ones wondering about the wife's name, and it's really tough to find the answer.

Why is Vulva called Vulva?

Even Georges has never made free to ask me that, it's so at odds and out of place in the talk of decent folk.

Why is Georges called Georges? Why is Paul called Paul? Why is Brownie Brownie, or why do we call Blossom Blossom?

It's like when they're born, the way the first time you see their mug the names come into your head and you just say "Blossom" or "Louise" straight off, though you've never thought of it before, for it's the name suits them, and there's no call to think women come by theirs any other way.

All the ones you see off their farms, they get the urge to make free and try every angle to come trampling and poking noses into the privacy of mine: "It's not much of a life, is it, with the wife away?" they go to me, grinning like someone had told them what we do in bed but hardly ever, and to crown it all: "One of these days we'll have to stop by and split a bottle," inviting themselves to come meddling and poking into my business, and to leave myself time to think up some excuse I tell them thanks like good manners requires, when Georges that's always alert with ears cocked he throws in his monkey-wrench: "Whenever you like," he gets in before me. "We'd like that, wouldn't we Paul?"

And after I say yes we shake hands and we goes our ways.

18

Evenings when there's a big wind you have to check the tarps on the hay before they blow off and the windows in the cow barn and the sheds to make sure nothing's lying about that could cause falls or damage or harm the good shape of the farm. You have to calm the animals that hear the roar of the wind threatening them all uneasy.

"Don't you worry, ladies," I go to them affectionate, "there'll be no wind from outside getting in here to send you tumbling: here there's Paul to protect."

I run my hand over their rumps, and don't they start masticulating with their jaws and tearing at the hay. There's none better than me at winning their trust. A hundred times I've tested and a hundred times I've proved the mastery I have over them: instinctive I know how to stroke to calm them down and where to pat, and intuitive I find the right word when the wee ones is scared, or when in winter they long in their souls for the open meadows, or are too lazy to shift in their sleep. In my hands there's a good fluid I've had from birth, without me ever trying to find out or explain or understand what goes on in my head, or what they make of it, the cows.

When I've calmed them proper I go to look in the kitchen what Georges is stewing up for us, for there's famine in my gut and night coming down stops us from going on.

In the kitchen Georges is there all right, but he's sitting at the plum with his elbows on the table and already glasses brimmed up for three, seeing aside from himself there's two off neighbor farms.

"Sit down, Paul, have a glass," he goes to me like the boss on this farm was Georges and Paul was the Portuguese and I needed his permission, and he says: "Cheers, here's to you!" and when I've brimmed up mine we raise them and empty them.

These two, I know who they are, though there's never been any excuse for stopping in or socializing. I don't know how it is, but it's no use never showing no interest, never being curious nor a gossip nor a nosey-parker nor a gabber, you always end up knowing the names of them from near by, and even if you've never gone visiting on their farms nor seen what it's like you know how many machines there is, how many cocks and hens, and how much cash, and if the wife is dark or fair, and how she's stacked up front, and so on: there's Martial of the local council that on top of his herd looks after the roads, cleaning up along the sides and driving the snowplows, and the other is Jean-Robert that has two tractors and pollutes the river, owns a big property, and rakes plenty into his money-box, and has the false blonde wife.

They let on they've come by chance and it was just my man Georges shouted so friendly over the gate to come in a while for some plum, and it was him brought them in.

"A grand idea, right?" Georges he says with a laugh, taking a swig. "For once some good company for a chat among men."

First we talk about Georges. There's a pile to say about Georges, enough to keep jawing for years, and they never dry up on the subject, though it's a meager one and not that fascinating. Maybe it's him encourages the talk about his person, and it's him starts it off again when we don't know what comes next. He's never been shy at displaying himself out in the open, he's never had inhibitions like them that says to themselves: "I'm going too far there," or maybe: "No one's interested in that," or: "I reckon I'm crossing the bounds of indecency there."

No, Georges he shows himself naked to his soul, he tells the four walls secrets another would keep hid till the grave, and he explains things about his life no one ever asked for nor no one wants to hear from him.

The two of them figure that for a brown person just recent out of Portugal he's adapted great to the climate and the rain, and he's mighty attached to the local traditions, due to his liking for the plum and his sociable nature.

Martial he questions how many days it took to get here, and Georges says air is a speedy means of transport and the longest part was in this country getting all the way to the farm, seeing there's only a rare bus goes by once or twice a day. Martial wants to know too what it's like, his village, if there's cows and if maybe there's enough cash for a machine? Georges he laughs for he lives in a city so big the people is millions, so in the street there's no one you know when you go out, and when he was little he came from a different place than the Portugal country, away on the far side of the ocean, a place called Brazil, if that rings a bell for us maybe?

Well we all leave a gap of silence, and Jean-Robert he tells how last year he took the plane, him and his wife, and the two of them they spent Christmas on this island together.

"Without the kids," he explains to us, "and at the sea, near paradise on earth."

I try to picture with Vulva on a plane or in the sea: it'd feel real strange to be lost off all by yourself with a wife and have to talk for conversation.

Martial he tells too how once he took the plane all the way to the Balearic country, and Georges he knows the place, so the two of them discuss, and Jean-Robert and me together we don't know what to say, so not to sit there gawping at one another we brim up the glasses again, and then the three of them jaw on about the cuts of planes and the kinds that work good and the kinds that go down.

"Me, I can do without the planes," I speak up, "for there's our animals here, and work for all of us, his farm for each, and the hay we need for the good life the Lord gives us," but the others they never turn an ear to what I'm saying, and they go: "Cheers!" and we all empty our glasses down, and then after that I can't remember so good how the chat went.

After that, if I'm not mistook, it was the time Georges was talking about women, for the two asked if he was married, and what she's like, his sweetheart, and where has he got her picture, and where could you see her?

Fortunate the young ones come to stir me, for they're calling for their supper, and it's late for God's sake, so I cut them two or three pieces of bread for their portions and the same with the cheese and I dole out in the bedroom.

When I come down again Georges is still on about the women, spouting about the couple and eternal love, about women's needs and the line to follow to have respect between intimates. Then I feel like a gall rising, and powerless to stop myself, with that inner laugh that drives your mouth to mischief, I put the question: "And I hope you told them you're not even married and there's no woman waiting for you back in Portugal, for you're toasted too dark, front and back?"

"Oh no!" the two of them go, but not Georges, he never says a thing, and then Martial he asks: "But in the photo then, who was that exactly?"

And Georges says with a laugh he was playing a little joke and she was his sister, the dark girl, but anyway he's had lots of women already and he has no problem finding one if the want comes on him. But when he looks it's like a bull going after the red.

"And you, Paul," Martial he asks, "how's she doing, the wife?"

Now there's a subject calms things, for the two stop slurping up the bottoms of their glasses and forget about their fidgeting and rubbing their noses, foreheads, stomachs, and chins, and they put on an air like they're not interested, but you can feel the itch in them to get me talking.

"Well," I say calm, "it's not going too bad, thanks for the concern."

But Georges he won't be happy till he gets me on his horns: "It hasn't always been easy, right Paul?" he goes with a wink and the two of them lean forward and wait on me to unload.

Georges he thinks I'm ashamed due to the disappointments and misfortunes Vulva brings me marital-wise, but I've no embarrassment on that account, and if I could tell Georges, or maybe let him guess, there's no reason to keep close-mouthed to ones off neighbor farms that is nearer in their souls than any Portuguese and far more apt to understand and grasp what you think. So I'm just setting to open up and tell about Vulva when Jean-Robert he bursts out, not able to hold back any longer, and he says: "She's called Vulva, your wife, right?"

And Martial he expands: "A real peach."

You'd fancy they was itching to know all about Vulva. "So where is she now? And when's she coming back?"

"A real peach," Martial goes again, and he thinks it's a shame they never see more of her, and Georges isn't happy with that turn of the chat for he throws more water on the oil: "If there just wasn't them problems . . ." he goes in my direction, with a sigh like there was a weariness on him, and he adds: "Oh, guys, if you only knew," with his mournful look, and they look curious, but Georges he turns to me: "It's not my place to speak, it's personal," suggesting it's up to Paul to reveal it.

First I take the bottle and I brim up our glasses with prune to lubricate our gullets, and then I stick my elbows out in front to show how I tackle it, and I start to talk, but I just go: "Vulva . . ." and I say again: "Vulva, uh, Vulva . . ." and the others come over awkward for they say: "Maybe we should go?"

But Georges he reckons there's no need, for I'm just concentrating and it's a bit emotional, and after a while it'll pass off, and he asks: "You okay Paul?" like to show them he's concerned, but back of it he's mean.

Me, that Vulva, when I think of her, when people want me to talk about her, or sometimes out in the field where I'm working, the first picture comes into my head is the big ball in her belly, under the belly-button all shoved out, and then the noises in the bedroom when she won't let you sleep. Then right out of the blue and in the flush of the plum I say, never even giving a thought: "That ball, it's this big," and I show with my hands the size of three oranges.

"Like a couple of plums," goes Martial.

"What ball are you talking about?" Jean-Robert he asks, and Georges he can't wait to tell the details of the whole story and describe even the colors like he'd seen it personal, so these two end up knowing all about it better even than Vulva herself that spawned the ball.

The subject that fascinates them is to know how they're going to get it out, but Georges he says that's been taken care of, it's gone already, and then they wonder what will they do with this piece they've cut out of her belly.

Georges says in his opinion they'll slice it up on a slide and study the slices through some apparatus, for they have micro-scopes and a whole laboratory, but I doubt they'll waste precious moments when they could be treating the balls in other patients. Martial he reckons they'll put it in a big garbage bag and maybe there'll be other bits and pieces off other people in it too, bits of legs and knuckle bones covered with flesh, and who knows maybe even bits of brain, and Jean-Robert he says out just like that for sport maybe they'll feed it to the dogs, and that only gets a laugh out of Martial and Georges and himself, but not out of Paul.

Paul sudden he feels a sour tide rising in his craw like a brine, but he never lets on, he just goes like a polite person off to the gents, but the tide flows over and spurts out on the ground and all over the side of his shoes, green.

Then they all stand up, and it's Georges to scrape off the ground and bring Paul up to bed, and meantime the other two leave.

19

And it's one of them mornings you rose with the dawn, and you drink the hot coffee from the thermos around ten, and then Georges he comes back stubborn to nag on about Vulva.

We're standing in our boots, and it's wet even under the overhang of the barn where we've taken shelter for our heads.

"I wonder if there's still diesel in the tractor," I say to the farmhand to take his mind off the wet and make conversation, just to have a wee jaw in the meantime and brighten things up, all but the sky.

"Yeah, maybe," Georges he answers, but he's turned his eyes down and never gives the tractor a look, just the dark puddles spilling over.

"We'll have to patch up a few shingles here and there," I go again, pointing to get him to look, but he dandles his head, so I smell the rat and ask right out: "Is something wrong?"

Georges he lifts his head up again and shakes it, with the drops: with him everything's fine, he says, it's just on account of Madame Vulvia he has a little worry eating at him. He stirs his foot about in the big puddle and never says another word, so it's for me to say: "So that's what's wrong then?"

Just about that, Georges he says, except he's had this notion too, but he's not sure if it'll please me or maybe make me angry, that it'd do Vulvia good to have a visit, a short little visit in her room in the hospital, and it'd only take an hour, or maybe only fifty minutes if you go straight and never stop off. For it's ages now we've had no news, and if we don't know what's happening maybe there's something bad the doctors aren't letting on.

Georges he waits for the answer, maybe he fancies he can fool me with his cock and bull about a trip and that I never see it's an excuse for playing mouse on the farm when the cat's away, so I list the whole catalogue off for the Portuguese to show he's easy to see through: "There's still the hens," I tot up for him on my fingers, "and the cows to be fed, and the grain silos, and washing out the bins, and the beams and the carpentry, and weatherproofing the roof and putting up the wire, and . . ."

But the Portuguese he cuts in: "Between now and winter there's time!"

"But the animals," I bawl in his face, "they've no time!"

It's true in the end Georges begins to rile you with his new ideas, like you could ever leave the farm for even an hour to go chasing after some Vulva.

"You should look about your respect," I bawl again, "on this farm I'm the master, and I'll never go to see Vulva, not never!"

Right, but I calm down when I see Georges' face all full of fright and his nostrils spread with terror, though sometimes it's a satisfaction to spit out in one go all that's been stewing in you from way back.

But Georges isn't done yet, and even after the scolding he plucks up to say if I agree he'll just add something to finish up, and he doesn't expect I will, but he says he thought it could maybe be for him to go, for without him, Jorge, the farm can still run perfect, seeing the boss is on the job.

That's the kind of bullshit he churns in his head all day when he's working! He's still thinking about his Vulvia and in his head he's canoodling and making sweet with her with never a thought for our animals nor the interest of the farm: he has his mind still on them grand thighs, and it's that keeps his humor up, even with the extra work he has with the young ones and the cooking and rising earlier by half an hour than we're used. That ball in her, it never disgusts him and nothing stands in his way, for Georges even in that hospital that stinks of Mercurochrome he still feels the urge to get his taste of Vulva.

You'd fancy that all the while these thoughts is whirling in my head Georges is watching the signs, for he says it's just to be useful and there's no need to agree if maybe it would cause upset or a problem. Besides, he has another thought running through his head: it's the notion he should go, not in his own personal function, but in the function of her husband Paul that's far too busy and has sent Jorge to bring her a note where he's put his hopes in writing. What do I think of that, asks Georges, don't I think it's a good idea?

"Maybe yes," I grant, "but out here there's no paper and no ink nor pens nor pencils for writing."

It gives me a real kick and laughing up my sleeve I can cross Georges and throw out his notion, letting on all the time I'd have accepted gladly except unfortunate there's a lack of materials, though I can hardly write or draft out long sentences, just read a bit and sign my name at the end: *PAUL*.

"No problem," Georges he says: he has brought all the necessaries with him in his suitcase, for they can always come in handy and Georges is never caught without a pen that works and a good wad of paper, for you can never know when the urge to write comes on.

We go in by way of the glasshouse. I'm hoping due to the mess Georges he'll never be able to find paper nor pencil and not start laughing when he sees how the words come all squinched up in my writing. Georges, he's a left-hander, he's written with his left even since he was a baby, he says, and he doesn't know how he got that way. And then he asks what way I write, me Paul.

"Well I've never real checked the way I write," I answer Georges, "no more than I've ever paid attention to see if I milk with the left or the right or some other way," and, to cut his cackle I go: "I do everything by nature, just like she made me." And I turn the other way for him to see the subject's closed.

Georges he brings out a pen and nice paper like fresh butter, clean and spotless, and envelopes, it's to send to my lady he laughs, and he proposes we do the writing in the kitchen for there's no room nor comfort in the glasshouse.

In the kitchen there's crumbs, but with a good swipe of a cloth I send the little mites flying till there's not one left. Now is no time for playing games, Georges he says, it's no time for sport, it's time for figuring out what to write to the lady, and it's no time to be yawning either.

"Sit up straight," he says, "and try to hold the pen between your two front fingers, and set to writing."

It's no use gritting your teeth and clenching your hands and all that, there's nothing comes.

"Think a little of your lady," he says, Georges, making free to put himself inside my head. "Just think a bit how she's lovely and the tender feelings that come when you think about her hair and her looks and the rest."

Georges he squinches up his eyes a little to show how it's done: for example you might say—but I'm free to do what I like and write the message my own heart wants to send her: "My Chicken" or "My Dear One" or "My Angel," it depends what you say to her in bed at night when there's just the two of you together, but that's our own business, and after that you could put: "How's things?" or "I miss you," or "I love you," in Portuguese to say something original, or another good thing maybe would be to put: "Come home soon darling, for without you I've lost my taste for life."

What do I think of that? Georges he asks, and does the Muse visit me when he gives me ideas?

Well, we've no call for no visitors to bother us, I tell Georges, there's enough to reflect about already, what with the soul and the page blinding white when you stare. It's all fine words, but nothing comes out right, for the page stays empty and my fingers go numb, they're gripped so tight on the pen. Georges he says he guesses it poses a bit of a problem, so why don't I just put what he says and do like what they call a dictation in school? But the spelling he can't help me with, he's never learned it for the language.

"It's fine with me," I reply, and I go to put a letter, but then there's a new problem, for a blob drops off the nib when it's set on its point and the page is ruined from the black juice coming from the bladder. So Georges he doles out another page, but the same thing happens again and the pen drops another big blob, and then another page, and then another, till Georges points out I'm pressing too brutal heavy on the tip.

Me, I don't claim to know much about pens, and I haven't enough bumptious pride to say to myself inward: "This here Portuguese is getting on my nerves with his wordings. He always fancies he's better than everyone else, the god damn darkie."

You can let someone tell you things when you hold the mastery, even a joker with a big gob that's anyway no more than a tiny mote in the life-story of a Paul but always fancies he knows what's right to do about a letter or a wife or a farm.

Already he's on his way back from the glasshouse carrying a pile more paper.

"Quit daydreaming now," says Georges, "and get to writing some sentences."

He starts talking to me like I was Vulva, and if he says "darling" it's not me he means, it's her, and it muddles you having to forget it's not me he's talking to but me talking to Vulva through Georges.

"My Dear Vulva," he starts off, and the words come slow at first but then fast: "Back here on the farm we hope you will come home soon to remain forever with me and the youngsters together and you will never go away to the hospital again. In the nights I miss you and dream I am holding you in my arms and . . ."

"Whoa, that's enough," I say to Georges, "I'm left away behind."

Me, all I've written is "My dar . . ." and then the fingers started to hurt. If he doesn't mind, I say to Georges, I'd rather write by myself whatever comes into my head, and if he went outside it would be good too, for he's a hindrance to thinking fresh.

"Okay, if you want," says Georges, but you can feel he's keeping an eye, for after he goes out he comes back through the door saying to take care not to break the nib on him, and then he comes back inside several times to see if there's a shortage of paper or if it's finished, so at last I say: "Go and see if the youngsters is outside," and Georges he's forced to go, for there's no one but me can give orders around here and it's him has to obey, and it was me decided to stay by myself to work out the writing of this letter.

What can you say to her, Vulva, when you never think of her? Me, in the end I've forgotten she exists, and what difference to me if she goes off to the hospital to have her belly sliced open or her varicose veins shrunk: I don't give a rat's fart, it doesn't squeeze a single big tear out of me nor get the snot-rag out of my shirt pocket, so she can stay away there till the next century if that's what she'd rather. At least it counts as much for me she's not around no more to give her jeremiahs after us and go complaining at us every time we open a bottle or go on a wee binge.

"It's finished?" asks Georges, back with the glad tidings that this morning all the youngsters is out in the yard. So to get him out of the way I give the order to go and see after the animals and make sure there's nothing they need in the rain, and this time I hurry up.

"Dear Vulva," I want to put, but I remember that came from Georges, so I change and cross out "Dear," but then there's nothing left but "Vulva," and it's not right to only put the name, it doesn't feel right, so I write "Wife" to her, like maybe I'd have said chatting, and after that I wait for the inspiration, and all of a sudden it comes: "We've had a lot of rain on the farm these past days, but never worry. When you're back better from away there, there'll still be piles of work for you."

And I reflect to know if it's better to put "Kisses" or "A big hug," and there's even some that would maybe put "Hugs and kisses," but I'd be afraid Vulva might fancy I've gone soft in the head and when she comes home she'll just relax and take things easy, so I put: "See you soon," though I reckon there's no way we'll be seeing her any time soon, and under that I specify: "Paul, husband," so she knows who's speaking, and there's only a couple of blots.

And there you are, I fold the letter up real small inside the envelope, and to close I lick the filthy glue they put to poison you.

By luck I do it quick, for already Georges is there, back from the animals.

"You're finished?" the two of us say to one another simultaneous, and we answer together: "Yes," and then Georges asks what I've written and if I wrote something nice.

"Yeah, very nice," I say, and Georges he writes the address on the envelope, but with no stamp, for he's going to carry it, and he puts "Vulva" in big letters, with a capital V.

20

At around two the bus stops and Georges he jams himself in among the summer camp kids with his trousers all nice and well washed and clean-smelling, and you can see just his head making off across the countryside looking straight ahead and never turning round to send a goodbye or a wave.

Together we got ready the letter, the bag, the sandwich, and the piece of chocolate to give Vulva a treat, and he set off to the bus with Paul as far as the signpost for company. From there you can see the farmhouse and the lane leading in, and back of it you make out the lovely fields of alfalfa and hay, and the hills, and that's the road I take home again all peaceful, and I admire the splendor.

When I go into the kitchen there's still saucepans to scour, for I'd said to Georges: "Leave the dishes, for the bus is coming and you're not even ready yet," and there was no blame: he went to get cleaned up, washing off the sweat and frying oil you get on you when you try to cook proper.

On the table there's still the plates the youngsters left, covered with salad and scraps of meat in gravy.

"I've it all to clear away," I tell myself in my head: "There's the whole lot to wash, tidy up, and then go see to the animals and after that call about Jasmine . . ."

I can see all right what has to be done, but the intention stops dead right there and never reaches the arms and legs to make them budge. It's just I feel no keenness to get going nor say to myself: "Set to work! Now there's work to be done!" nor feel the pleasure you get breaking your back plowing or at the cows.

The only thing in my head is fancying Georges has been there and wondering what he can say to her and where he is right now that it's half past two by the watch. He'll be near the hospital, in her room, I calculate rough, he'll be saying hi and handing over the letter and he'll have started out for home, for he's coming on foot.

I notice to myself all the time how Georges spares himself and always gets the best deal: when we set off to the bull it's him sits up front gawping about him at the countryside and it's me drives, focused on the lines and seeing if there's maybe a car coming up in the mirror and gripping tight on the gear-shift. But when we get there it's Georges sets to work, like with the doctor that time, so it's him unloads the cow, and they all fall ass-backward like it was Georges had milked her himself and brushed her with the strength of his wrist all these past years.

It's of a rare selfishness, a Portuguese that sets himself up and even in the middle of dinner slips himself the good chicken thigh or a piece of meat no one else makes free to take, for there's only one left in the dish with nine half starved around longing for it.

Who'd have said no to taking off on a jaunt through the villages and the town or to the hospital even? Who can't see, from wherever he stands, the advantage of gallivanting about when there's work crying out to be done? But someone with conscience, someone that knows the honor of work, he stays stuck to the job, he keeps hard at it and never flinches, even if he's hatching ideas like anyone on this earth would: it's only human to say to yourself: "Today I'd like to go for a bit of an outing," or maybe: "I'm fed up gawping at the walls and mantels of this farmhouse." For all them things, even if you love them, even if you respect them, you can still be foolish enough to go off just like that just for the sport, even if you know you'll be homesick later and it's a false dream figuring it's greener across the fence.

Wherever you go there's always four walls and annoyances, and behind the door a face and red cheeks ready for a glass, and whatever you start to say you call on the same stock: if you ask "How's things?" the others always answer: "Fine, and yourself?" and if you say: "Looks like there's a change in the weather," the other says: "Summer's a dead loss this year," and you go back at him: "Ah, what's become of the lovely summers we had long ago, with the heat waves?" and always the other answers: "It's yon ozone hole at the pole," and when you go a bit farther, along comes another one: "Good day to you," he goes, "how's it going?" and we say: "Fine, and yourself? And he goes on: "There's a change in the weather," and you: "The seasons is all screwed," and on like that to the end with everybody using the same beginnings to get the words out, and that's why, when all's said, I'd rather keep on the farm instead of going to another man's place to knock back a few glasses playing cards and come home after the moon's up.

That's the way I chat to myself, imagining cues for me to bring up the conversation I want: "Hi Paul," I say to myself. "Hi yourself," I answer just to me. "You're working awful hard," I tell myself sincere. "That's right," I say just as frank, "there's not one can work like Paul. It's not like that farmhand Georges: you know right well he's just letting on he's slaving away, but the truth is he's just a dirty good-for-nothing," that's the way I yarn to myself for the sport.

The good thing about being on your own is you can talk all kinds of blather and cock and bull you wouldn't dare bring out for no one else's ears: when you're on your own you can relax and yarn away to yourself about all that's going on, and things can come up you're amazed to come on, like all the times Vulva occurs in my brain: "Oho, oho," I say to myself, "Paul, that's a real good-looking lady you have there!"

And I let on she's going past in her nightdress, across the doorway, just casting her shadow like the girl in the movie. "Oh go on," I answer back, "she's just a floozy like the rest!"

Then for example Vulva comes along and snugs up to get a stroking and the affection a hussy wants, and she cuddles close against me and you see she has the breasts transparent under the top so all the males around have their hands stuck in their pockets not to grab. It's cram-full of hungry males gawping, but it's me she belongs to, and I say: "Damn hay-bag," and I land her a good clout, and they see when she falls she's just a big fat old biddy with six brats at least that have flabbed out her belly and sucked

107

her tits down, and they all say: "She's just an old cow-pat all over flies. She's stale under that hide," and all sorts of such words that brings Vulva back humbled and obedient to her man. That's for an example of what I say, for sometimes it's different, and it's possible maybe no one notices I do things around here the way I want, or that Vulva looks changed, except since she's sick Vulva doesn't come to mind so often, for there's more important things to reflect on. There's thinking about the bedroom downstairs and chewing over the proper morality of using it again or not, and I say to myself: "What do you reckon, Paul, wouldn't that bedroom downstairs do great for a visitor's room or a parlor?"

"Of course," I answer, "but I've promised Pa, and I'm a son sticks to his word."

"Pa, he's long dead and gone already," I remind myself.

"Well, that's right, yes, fifteen years now," I calculate, "or even seventeen this March."

"You know what a son's honor is, my fine Paul," I congratulate, "but before your turn comes, you too think of your own."

You too think of your own! Well yes, it's true you have to think of them, the young ones that's the fruit of my loins and Pa's descendants and mine and his wife's too. Think of your sons! Now it's true all this time I've been caring about Pa, I've been caring about the farm and the animals and even about Georges, but I never gave a thought to the wee ones running around that's growing up and will soon be as good as men, fit to work on the land and set their hand to a pitchfork.

You could make a place in the bedroom downstairs for them to sleep decent or to welcome visitors and it'd still revere Pa's memory if you told everyone: "This was Pa's room that he had shut up out of selfishness, but Paul, thanks to his strength, for he's a man of character, he took it back into his own hands for the good of his offspring."

That's the reason I go in often to check the measurements and figure out what it could be used for. Inside I always turn on the electric just like Georges did, though I'd never made free to do that out of morality and reverence for the dead. There's still flies all over the floor and droppings, but it's not going in there like a woman with a floor-rag: you're there like an architect or a real decorator that knows at one look where to put a clothes-rack or a table.

In the corner, if the sheet's taken off, there's the color TV I once hid there due to Vulva's passion for pictures of far places. Me, I like TV and the pictures going by so you can even find out what the Chinese is saying when they're washing between their toes, but at the outset of the marriage, when Vulva stayed out of bed for the soaps, I said: "It's them or Paul," and I made up my mind and I put the screen into its box under the cover that looks like an altar-cloth and into Pa's room, for he liked to watch matches and sports.

And while I'm in there checking the measurements and shifting a few bits of furniture about and hunkering down to check the skirting, what do I hear but a car driving in, so I take a squy out the shutter, and there's Georges real close in his best duds and a happy look across his mug, and a car that brought him.

"Hi boss," shouts Georges, to let this hussy that's getting out know where I'm watching them from, and I let on I'm glad to see them, opening the shutter wide and never hiding behind it.

"That was a grand idea to open it up at last," calls Georges, and he explained to his floozy how that room has been shut up from years back on account of the deceased, and I've reopened today, and with no boasting it's from him this idea sprouted, with her going "Oh! Oh!" all ecstatic like she was before the Holy Virgin.

"Yeah," I go cool and collected to no one in particular, "but it was thought of long before that," and I'm boiling inside wanting to stop his blabbing.

Georges he congratulates again and he says if I come outside he'll explain about this hussy and what she's doing in my yard.

She's Claudie, one of the neighbor wives, the one belonging to her husband Charles, for now I recognize her, only she has wavier yellow hair. It's due to the hairdresser making her beautiful, she explains, and when she laughs it's like the cackle of a dozen hens or the clatter of saucepans.

Georges he'd taken into his head he'd try to hitch, for on the road he said to himself: "All them cars driving by themselves, and Jorge here walking all alone."

So he stuck up his thumb and he had to wait patient, half an hour, three quarters of an hour, for someone seeing a brown guy at the side of the road that would take the chance of letting him onto their seat. And it was Claudie picked him up, and Georges he's never stingy and knows how to show gratitude, so he told her to come in for a drop of plum to thank her for her trouble. But Claudie she refused, for it was just natural and the least you could do, a service between neighbors, even if Claudie thought that tanned and brawny like he is it was some black man or a southern North African walking through illegal on his way to the border, but she's always been generous, she can't help herself, and she has no regrets, for Georges is a real funny guy.

She gives him a dig in the ribs with her elbow and laughs, and you can see her tongue. It seems Georges gets on like a house fire with the crazy hysteric, and he remarks what a good laugh you can have with the women sometimes, and he digs her back and they split themselves laughing like they was taking the mickey out of me. So I say solemn: "I don't think there's time for a drink, seeing there's that gray sky coming over to bring rain."

Georges he says yes, there's that sky all right, and for sure she must be off, and he puts on a serious look you'd fancy all sad and hangdog, and Claudie quits her laughing, for anyway she has no time to fritter for she has a farm too and a husband waiting for her that's very strict and has a shovel to clout her with, she says, and I just have to go off or look away for the two of them to go gawping at one another fit to burst. But I never leave them the opportunity: "Yeah, yeah, yeah," I go quick. "You'd better get going then," and I hold the car door for her, and out of politeness I show an interest in her husband: "My best to your husband Charles," I say to her friendly enough but never smiling in case she'd fancy she's popular and come for a return visit.

"I'll be sure to," she says, "and give my best to your lady too, that poor thing away in the hospital," and she makes a few signals to Georges and then she starts up the car, making far too much noise and enough fumes to gas the hens.

Georges after she's gone he turns round and makes to get changed for work.

"Sluts of hussies you can never get quit of," I go to get a rise out of him.

111

"Sometimes, yes," answers Georges, but nothing more, and there's nothing forcing him.

"Them nosey hussies, they come poking around the farm, and they can't tear themselves away without a good shove in the ass," I develop more detailed: "They just come to find out information and then go broadcasting your private business all over," I'm making him feel bad for the betrayal, on account of Vulva.

"I saw Vulvia in the hospital," says Georges, to sidetrack.

"I'd hope so," I interrupt, "but now's no time for chatting about it, it's not peaceful when there's a rush on"—even though I'm longing to know how much longer we can stay carefree on the farm.

Georges he looks at the sky and says he doesn't reckon it's setting to pour on us.

"Well me neither," I let out, "I just mentioned the sky to get that one to clear off, but right now the work's in here." So I show the open window and through it you can see the walls, the frames, the dried flowers and the TV and the bed still ready made up like it's waiting for someone.

21

We set the TV where it should always be in the best of homes: in the living-room, in front of the table, in the place where Georges says down there where he comes from in Portugal he has put his too, though ours is bigger.

"That's no surprise for me," I tell Georges. "I'm not surprised they make littler ones down south."

And I ask what it's like, if it has colors and how many channels.

Well Georges he's never counted, but he can say there's over thirty he gets by the satellite.

"Of course it's by the satellite," I laugh at his lack of wit. "Surely you don't think the people is there inside that little box!"

Just then by luck, there's a goal, for Georges he can't stand being laughed at or being made a fool of, but he has no time to answer before I shout "Goal!" and I hug him.

Normal that's not a thing I like to do, hugging someone else. Normal I keep calm with one eye on the plum, but since we've been watching on together and fans one against the other it comes like from deep down, as if I'm the winner when Real Madrid gets a goal. Georges, he's not keen on hugging, it puts him off his orbit and stops him looking out for when they're setting to put in the next one and even up the score.

All the time we're watching and passionate against one another Georges tells about Vulva and what he did on his visit.

When he got on the bus he noticed the chewing gum on the seat, but by good luck old and dry already, for otherwise Georges' nice duds, all brand new, would have stuck to the bus, but even so out of principle he hands the summer camp kids a lecture. And afterwards in the little town (not a pretty one, by the way), he found the hospital and never needed to ask, for he has a feel for direction, Georges, and aside from the modern church and the station and the bars and the two supermarkets and the school and the apartment buildings there's nothing special in that little mite of a town.

"Yeah, but there's the church windows and the fountain," I say out of importance, "and places with coatings from the centuries."

He's surprised to hear that, Georges he says, for he had the chance to look about and he tried to find History, for he always likes that, but he found nothing worth the trouble of looking.

To cut short, Georges heads off inside the hospital and spends an age hunting, for it's so big and high and spread over a lot of floors. Hers is No. 60, a door like the others, but special all the same. It's a funny feeling coming to it to fancy you know already what it's hiding, that Vulva is lying right there on the other side, and you feel your throat knotted tight out of fear and emotion, and you're nervous.

"Get on with it, make it short," I hurry him on, for at this slug's pace there's enough left to tell till after half time.

Then at last he knocks, Georges, and in place of the thin voice expected it's a strange loud one that goes: "Yes?" for him to go in, and Georges tells himself for sure he's made a mistake, but it's too late for pulling back, so courage and in he goes.

Oh, but first I have to know, and he has to go back to make sure the picture in my head is real, just the way it was, he forgot to say he bought flowers before he went up, a nice bunch of red roses with the cash I lent him for an emergency, for Georges he thought it's a poor policy to cut back on flowers that maybe would give her courage and show she's loved and respected, even if he was forced to go over and add funds out of his own pocket, but when there's love, he thought, Paul's not one to count the cost, and he's out ten francs if I've the cash on me.

Okay, so I give him the cash I've put aside in the dresser, eight fifty, with no objection, though for flowers the fields is full of them, but aside in my mind I make a note to deduct from his pay, and he goes on: oh, if only I'd seen him, the fine looks of him, Georges, all handsome in his best duds, with lovely roses that prick, but Georges he knows how to hold the stem between the pricks, and modesty apart even that crabbed nurse that has seen plenty of visitors looked at him kind and near smiling.

There I ask him to get a move on, for I don't give a rat's fart about any roses or his fine suit and all that, with all respect to

Georges, so I ask: "So what about the room?" to get the movie rolling, though it's a dud.

Inside the room there's this woman, not a nice one, the nurse Georges still has said nothing about, though she's the first thing he sees going in, for she's standing there: she announces she's doing treatment and says to Vulvia that's hid behind the white curtain: "Here's your husband come to see you at last," and asks Georges to wait a minute, but Georges he protests, he corrects right off he's not Paul but Georges, though he could have kept his trap shut.

"Yeah, yeah, yeah," I say to Georges, "that's not the real important thing. What's important is if she's staying or she's coming back, and when."

"Wait a minute," says Georges: he doesn't like telling out of order with no details, and I have to represent like I was there myself. You have to picture the way things happen, and for that there's need of a description of the room.

In Vulva's room there's another woman's room as well: a blue lady in her bed-sheets that's maybe ninety, and she's so decrepit-looking you can't tell if she still has her hearing. Georges bids her good morning like you do out of politeness, with a few words to show sympathy too, and all unsuspecting he goes over to listen when she talks, this lady, and at the start you're sympathetic but it takes no time to catch on she sticks like flypaper and all the while she's gabbing away about diseases and treatments you're caught, and you'll be a dried-up corpse before she's done.

By luck, the nurse coming to get the flowers (to put in a vase, she said, though you hardly saw them again), she said to him: "I'll leave her to you," and Georges drops the old lady, to hell with good manners, and goes lifting the veil to see Vulva in the bed.

"How does she look?" I let out, in spite of me swearing I'll let him see no curiosity nor interest for that one.

She's stretched out lying back deep, he says, Georges, with her eyes closed and only her legs moving, and it gives you a strange feeling to see her like that all slack and pale so you'd fancy for real she was dead except you can see her chest beating and lifting, and he talks so strange I take my eyes off the game to see if in truth he's dropping a tear.

At that point he sat on the bed to chat with her.

"On the bed?" I go to Georges, just to keep a rein on him, but Georges pays no attention and carries on with his telling.

Madame Vulvia she looks at him and she says nothing out of her mouth, she just talks with the eyes, and the eyes cry out she's hurting.

Georges he goes silent: it's a moment to reflect on the screen, especial for there's lots going on in front of the goal, but it's just a false alarm, so he goes back to the room. Then he looked at her, Georges, and with my unspoken permission he took one of her hands, and he told her by heart what he knows we feel in our gut, me, the youngsters, and the farm. He told her: "You mustn't cry," and: "Never despair," and: "Greetings from all, and your husband's thinking of you."

Then he thought: "The letter!" and he gave her the envelope. Vulvia read it and she cried, out of emotion Georges he figures, and then she described the ray treatment for him and the hard time she had after they operated for the ball.

Right then comes the goal, a fantastic one, a header into the top of the net, so we stand up against one another yelling, and after that when we sit down we've forgot what we was doing in that poor room of Vulva's and where we'd left off. Georges he says it's a shame to cut short at the best place, and if I've no objection he'll pick up from a little earlier, right where the nurse says: "I'll leave her to you," and goes out with the flowers she's robbing.

Then Georges he sits down on the bed to look at Vulvia and seeing there's no chair.

"On the bed?" I go to Georges for a second warning, just to put him at his ease, and he picks up the story again.

"How are you doing?" Georges he asked.

"She's not doing so great," comes from the blue lady, but Vulvia says in the thin wee voice we know from the farm: "I'm doing fine thanks Georges."

"Is there anything you need?" he asks again, Georges, for he knows that's the right thing to say to sick people getting treated, and Vulvia she said: "Nothing, thanks," though the lady said in a loud voice from her bed: "Didn't you say you needed undies?" and seeing Vulvia was upset at the interference Georges pulled cross the veil so the old blue biddy couldn't spy on what was going on. But even through the curtain she can still hear, and she calls him out answers, so Georges and Vulvia talk in whispers.

"Oh is that so?" I go then, to show I'm sharp and not easy to fool.

Vulvia looks real wore out in the face, with the lips sticking to the teeth for lack of liquid. She's all shriveled up, and it's queer to see her scalped like she is, so you'd fancy she was real old, almost like a granny, all sunk in. Around the eyes it's black, around the nose it's red, and on the forehead the skin is sagging loose, but it's not serious she says when he asks, it's due to the substance that's crucial for the belly but that she tolerates bad in her body.

He tried to talk about the farm, but her eyes start filling as soon as he talks, so quick Georges tells some stories to make her laugh, for there's no one better at injecting an atmosphere with humor and gaiety.

Right then who does he see coming but seven white doctors in coats. You can tell they're doctors just from the color of their badges and seeing how hard they're thinking, serious all the time and frowning like there was no sunshine and summer was done. They pull back the curtain, never even telling Georges good morning, paying him no attention like he wasn't sitting there or you could see through him, and when Georges moves the stout doctor makes him go out for five minutes, just for the time they're examining.

Close by there's chairs and newspapers and magazines, and reading them Georges learns things about the King of Spain and about Holland, a lovely country to be sure.

"Yeah, but what about my Vulva?" I ask.

It's not often I call her "my," and more often it's "that big lump," or "that floozy," or "that sow," except when the opportunity comes up when you need to show your ownership, that you've a stake in the matter and you're master over her.

"Wait for the rest," he says, Georges.

Before Georges was done with Holland, the beautiful country of tulips, the door opened and the docs came out. Georges got up and went after them to ask news of the surgery.

"It's the husband," said one.

"Has he been informed?" asked another one, but no one answered, and then they told Georges she can come home soon, but right now they're in a hurry, and off they head to another room, No. 66, if Georges remembers right. But: "Just a minute," says Georges to the doctors, so they stop, and he lets on he's the husband, please forgive him but it's only due to the importance it lends for getting heard, for if Georges had said: "I'm Georges, the farmhand" or: "I'm just the worker from Portugal" they'd have laughed in his face and never told him a thing about the ball.

But then the doctors is all impressed and they look at one another and don't know what to say, you could feel their embarrassment in front of Georges, till the stout one says in a few more days she'll be going home, and the other white ones go yes all relieved, and they dig their hands deep in their pockets and wheel left after the leader.

It was then he went back in to see Vulvia, but she'd gone back to sleep, so Georges waked her to tell her the news that just a few more days and she'd be away back on the farm again, in her own bedroom. It always brings tears in her eyes when there's talk of the farm, and it's just at the wrong moment that thief of a nurse comes back carrying the flowers.

"What's going on here?" she asks, not looking like she's amused, and it's no use Vulvia telling her she's very content and feeling a huge joyous happiness at seeing Georges, at his big hand on top of hers, and that Georges makes her feel better with his chat (and he's making nothing up, he'll swear on the farm), but the nurse is angry and she's setting to throw him out for she figures he's wearing her out with his gabbing.

"Big deal," says Georges, "we did worse than that on the farm!"

So then comes a gap when Georges has to stop, where he has to drop his story due to certain details that escape my memory, and after we've established it was really nothing he was referring to, that it was just one day I was out mowing they once chatted for an hour, him and Vulvia, Georges swears, so I let him go on in spite of my suspicions.

Being as the sour old nurse is insisting he's got to leave and is standing there waiting, Georges he gives Vulvia a hug, assuring again it's from Paul with his undying affection, and he walks straight along the road till he sees a car stop and it's Claudie, and she drives him to the farm, and that's the end of his story.

Then I go over to turn off the TV: the match is long over, not an interesting one at all but a bit of a dud, dull as dishwater, for the final score is one apiece.

22

The thing is, these days there's no Georges to be seen about the house no more. He's off as soon as the job comes up against the dark and it's no use fancying you can work on. Then Georges he lays down his shovel or his spade, or the big dung-fork, or he gives a slap on the cow's rump if it's after milking, or on the side of the tractor, and he says: "I think this day's about done."

To which I answer always: "Just one little stab more," and I carry on a bit longer with the spade, or the shovel, or the tractor, or I milk two minutes more just to see when he'll crack and ask for mercy: "Are we going for supper, to see what the youngsters is cooking?"

And for another thing, he's stopped making our portion too. "It takes too much time," he says. "It's a waste," is his excuse with respect to the time he spends filling saucepans for us, so after that the young ones, the ones that's capable, they make the eggs, the rice pudding, and the stewed fruit, and Georges, as soon he's done

raking up his plate, with never a thought for the dishes or anything else, can say: "I'm off for a bit of a walk," and there's never
hair nor hide of him about the house till the next day.

At first I thought maybe the bother was the TV, seeing it stays
on all evening for the education value, and I asked Georges: "Is it
the TV bothers you?"

"No way," Georges he said, the TV's no bother: he likes to watch
the soaps and what's on the channels. No, he just has a kind of
need to stretch his legs in the evenings, for it catches him here,
says Georges, pointing to his hips, and it sort of drives him to
exercise them to keep his condition.

"Well if you're not wore out from walking again evenings," I say
to let him know the weariness he's piling on himself and that he
shouldn't complain if maybe a little extra effort is asked in the day,
but then I let him go, for I don't give a fig what he's up to.

On TV after the news there's movies, the kind Vulva's wild
about but that first you never want to watch but then you wait
curious to know what's coming next. Well I always say on TV you
can see some good stuff, but there's strange stuff on the channels
too if you happen across them. Some sights disturb you, so you
push the buttons fast, any old way, and the box makes the channel
change automatic, but never so quick that your eye doesn't pick up
the pictures that unsettle and roil you all night in your dreams.

Me, them's things I never let out external: it's subjects should
never be talked about nor ever told out open, and never let stir
up the notion of what can go on in the night when you've one
in bed with you and it comes like an imperial surge of nature
swelling in the body that sets you impregnating before you even
realize. I've never let out a word about such things, never a re-

mark, out of honor, and Vulva's learned that and no mistake, for at the outset of the marriage she'd say when the business was done: "That was no use," or: "That hurt," or: "Maybe I felt something." But since I landed the slap and the warning that them's things to be left unspoken and there's no words for them, she never says the like no more, she never says a thing and she just shows with sighing or tears but never with expressions or words that cheapen and soil the works of Love, for there's people that say, and anyone's free to disagree, there has to be Love, and the body and the hands should be full of it to go feeling, and above all setting at it, for if there wasn't no one would do the thing men do to women.

But me, always I tell myself: "It's not right to call it Love, seeing you feel nothing in your soul, just the urge to go at her and let her have it."

It's Rage or Fury we should say, or better just keep our traps shut and say nothing, letting on we never do such a thing, and if Georges sometimes talks about it it's better to let on you tolerate in case he goes sticking his nose into your bed-sheets again.

Yet I know what it feels like, the way it is when you love: you keep squying at her and sighing, you have the everlasting fear something bad might occur to damage her about the horns or make you call the vet. You feel you're responsible, and you think about that all the time, even evenings, and there's nights you can't sleep out of Love. When you see her it's like a stiff one you've knocked back and starts warming like sunlight through the gut and arms. But Vulva she never does that, she's never sent no warmth or weakness through my arms, she's never caused none of that restlessness that keeps you awake when the moon's out, for she never inspires no affection but just the anger to land her a clout and figure you'll go at it sharp and finish it off presto.

At this juncture in my reflecting I hear Georges coming in and going through the kitchen to rob something to drink.

"Back already?" I call at him, to show I've heard and I'm aware of his presence.

"Yes, back already," says Georges and he sits down alongside in front of the TV with a clear glass in his hand, and you can't tell from any smell if it's hard stuff or just water.

Me, it's Georges' own business where he's off to post haste at night across the dark and dim of the meadow, but if we wasn't away back of beyond with just a couple of roads and two or three roofs behind maybe it'd occur he's off chasing after some floozy, if you wasn't sure there's no lonely hearts around these parts just waiting for a man to fall in their laps.

"How was it?" I ask, though I've no notion what I'm talking about.

Georges he puts on a vague look and he answers: "Good, yes, good," but he's devious in the eyes.

On TV there's a movie starting, one of the late ones, all bare skin and screwing on women.

"Leave it a minute," says Georges when I pick up the little gadget for changing the channel, so I reprieve as long as there's no carryings-on on the screen.

"You're right to take care and stay on the road so the dirt doesn't stick to your shoes," I comment, inspecting his sole bottoms, and I add as well to investigate: "So it's not across the land you go walking evenings?"

Georges he never answers, for he's caught, sucked in by the way the woman in this movie is huddled in the porch with the man getting ready to come and kiss her on the mouth. "So who's it you go visiting then?" I go again, and as well it's to screen out the movie that he never notices the hand going over the sweater and grabbing what you should never on a lady.

"What's that, Paul?" he says, Georges, and the two of us look at the shocking spectacle, and I've to press to stop the machine. Georges, you'd fancy he'd landed off some other planet. He gawps about and asks why I don't like the movie, for I'm turning off at the best spot in the story.

"Too much pig-swill," I point out to teach the lesson, and I go back on attack: "So who's it you're going to see out there, Georges old pal?" talking like a kind father, all easygoing and indulgent.

"Oh, no one much," he answers.

"Come on, come on," I go joking, "spill the beans to your boss," though with no hope it'll work, for he's distrusting, but unexpected Georges gets set to open up in words: sometimes there's things you keep to yourself, for you'd rather, and you bury matters of intimacy, you shut them up inside, if I get his meaning, he says with a little laugh and a weariness on his lips, and then he leaves a whole minute's silence by the clock.

"But them things," I invent, "they never weigh heavy on the heart?" remembering the way Georges once put it to me that day I told Vulva's story, us sitting against the gate at lunch with our ham sandwiches on our knees.

Georges, he reflects for an answer with his eyelids down like he's dozing, and he says he's reflecting if it's his right to divulge, seeing he's not the only one involved, for there's someone.

"Someone?"

I'm all ears.

"Yes," he answers, Georges, but there's a hesitation in his head between on the one hand spilling the beans to his good pal farmer Paul, or saying nothing so as to leave the other party safe and trustful of the secrecy between them.

Another affair over a stolen hen or some such robbery, I suspect inward, and if Georges spills to me I'm off to the law, for a reputation gets tarnished for a speck and the dark stain stays on the farm for years, but first I slip in cunning: "You can go ahead, Georges old pal, for what goes in one of my ears comes straight out the other," but it's a lie: it's the very opposite, for I still have off by heart all the fables I learned in school.

"Agreed to tell," he says, Georges, but first I've to swear I'll not go spreading around, and I agree, and he asks what I'm swearing on, so I say: "The Bible," but according to Georges that's not solid enough of a guarantee, so I say: "On Vulva," but Georges still questions the value, the price I'm setting, so I suggest: "On Pa," and Georges accepts, just as I'm telling myself the old bugger's doomed if ever I go gabbing.

With my two hands up I pronounce the syllables out clear: "On my Pa, on the head of my begetter that's rotted in his coffin," and I go on with what I said over the grave, that there was a whole lot lacking in him, but he was Pa all the same, at which Georges finds it's dragging, and he figures it's valid as an oath without the rest, and we shake hands to show we're agreed.

Then Georges clears his throat: "Well here goes," he begins, "it's the story of the apple."

Does the riddle call for an answer or didn't I catch the whole thing? All innocent I say again, like I was distracted or hard of hearing: "You go away out there for what?"

Then Georges makes no further mention of the apple but he explains how the Bible tells what it was like the first time a young guy spotted a good-looking filly.

"I know all about Adam and Eve," I cut him short, and to show what's what I told all about the rib, the subsidiary birth, and the tempter coiled round the trunk among the leaves of the fruit tree, and Jehovah, and female weakness, and all the things they teach in school, so Georges he just has to rectify it's nothing to do with eating, it's about what's hidden back of the apple.

Do I catch the things he's trying to talk about without saying it out? Georges queries.

Well no, I can't get it real clear, so maybe he can explain further, just for dummies, I go with a laugh.

Well, when you talk about the apple, he goes, Georges, you're making a reference, it's like speaking about something else, or saying with an image a thing you'd like to bring out but don't want to soil with low words. "But about what?" I inquire.

"Well, that tasty apple," says Georges, "who was it showed it to her man?"

"It was that Eve," I answer, and then Georges explains how talking about the apple means Eve, signifying you hold love for a person deep in your gut. But it's no use me searching, for no one called Eve comes to mind, nor any other that might be on the look-out for a man.

"But what's she called?" I have to inquire then.

Ah, her name, says Georges, that's a thing he can't tell, for the lady doesn't want known she's consorting with Georges.

"Maybe it's yon Rose," I make up, for Rose from the shop she weighs a ton and she's old and ugly too, and it'd make no sense at all for a fellow like Georges to be carrying on with her.

"Yeah, Rose, maybe she's the one," I dig on purpose to rile him and make him cough up the name.

"A fine trunk of a woman," I remark, "and well larded up front," and I draw with my palms, with my arms out round at the elbows, and they're not excessive for the job, like it'd be normal to fancy Rose was lovely when she looks more like a stuffed pipe-bowl with twisty shreds spilling out the top.

Georges, he never answers, he holds back and just says: "Maybe and maybe not," and he gives a little laugh under his breath.

Likely he believes firm, Georges, that it's jealousy from knowing he has someone when Paul he has no one, or just the left-overs of one that's like a hospital cast-off. He reckons Paul is torturing himself at not knowing who Eve is, so to put an end I say: "It's real late," and I get up and head off into the dark to close the windows and shutters all round and show I don't give a rat's fart what he's up to, for late evenings there's a sleep comes over me.

23

Days when I can I head out sometimes across the land to smoke and work in my own way, and I work myself good and fast to my personal liking and free of the dawdlings of a farmhand with a jokey mouth that never wants to drink a health and shames you for putting some aside for yourself and knocking back a glass on your own.

Going over the land it's a dream to cover across in big strides, heading to the left or on the right if you like and knowing the field belongs to me, and the branches is mine, and every blade of grass for me, and the leafy thickets and the stones on the tracks if I like I can level out and concrete over or just shut the gates and no one will come in ever again.

I go straight over never thinking about the way: I go forward right across the grass till it says in my head there's a call to put my back in, so I set to and I put my heart to going hard and doing a grand day's work all through.

But this time by surprise I head off through the virgin forest that they call like that, it being all tangled thickets and bushes in thousands, and the youngsters come building huts in it.

Why am I headed to this side of the land, I ask myself, when there's never a thing sowed or planted under the branches? But I keep going and start reflecting about what Georges says, that the apple comes from Eve and that talking about the apple means keeping unspoken things you don't want to say out.

Georges he has a woman he loves and he goes to visit, and she calls him "Darling!" when he yokes with her and goes weepy when he leaves, Georges he has the power in his hands to get into her thighs whenever he fancies and pleases and he goes gallivanting by moonlight and never giving a thought for the farm, a woman that takes over his mind, so Georges is losing his and he's external to the cows and the fate of the farm, on Paul's land a Georges from away that steals any woman good for getting your hand into, and I'm thinking so hard I stray off and head into the trees never knowing where nor why, and I go in under the branches, and sudden there's midges and insects and mosquitoes that attack all at once, but you land them a few smacks and soon you feel nothing. There's a strange cracking under the trees, in the jumble of bushes where there's no path but just the dry stream I'm going along.

So Georges how did he go about finding himself that floozy, him that's big, tall, and browny-black like he is, and like a bull through the chest so you'd think a hussy would sooner take fright that he'd clout her and do her serious hurt and if he goes at her she'll dislocate, so he's not the sort you'd fancy could find women nor the kind you'd ever look at and say: "He's handsome!" or "That's a good-looking fellow!" or: "What looks that one has!" He's more of the dark sort that to start with you never know what to make of him due to him being so sooty about the face except for the eyes, and you never offer to call him "Monsieur," for you don't even know that one can talk.

But there up front all of a sudden in the woods real close there's a shifting and scrabbling, it's critters charging one another, it's animals fighting I suggest to myself, so I keep going, and it stirs a lot through the branches, and now there comes a moaning and then what do I see but Georges bare naked black and all tangled up with a woman stark hideous under his legs with the tits all twisted, and they're yoked together in the brushwood and kissing on their mouths, never mind the leaves sticking.

Oh the horror! I pull back oh the horror to look oh the horror that woman all tangled with Georges, it spins me round, tits legs oh no don't see don't look it's chasing me don't think it catches up to me again tits crotch again when I run away far out of the woods with my lungs out of breath.

You do right, you manage to do right on this earth, you force yourself to map out the proper happy life for a farmhand, you think everyone does like you've taught, and then you see him tits and legs, you want to give trust but this Portugal he comes fouling the ground on you; you want to give work and they fritter away the day and the prosperity of the farm; one you think is proper upstanding and clean like your own soul, he's a wrecker, he tramples you and instigates you into his plots. Claudie's tits, they're little like pears, never seen such tiny pears, with her husband Charles sitting at his beer on the porch in his yard and never suspecting nothing, you couldn't see nor feel a thing of it just from looking that she's a liar and goes wanting to get diddled, and doing it in the open cool as custard, the thing you never make free to do in your own bedroom.

At that juncture of my thinking I find myself sitting at the table before the open bottle swigging straight from the neck. At this time of day a farmer should be outside hunkered at the milking or up on the tractor, but here you sit debating if you should hold on to that big Georges or pack him onto the next bus and spill the whole story to Charles.

First it has to stop, the seeing, seeing, and seeing over, for if it keeps coming back endless it'll leave no time for deciding. For it's not the easiest thing to decide just and moral, away back of beyond on a farm when there's no one but yourself in the world for matters of conscience. In Pa's day you discussed, and when disagreements come out open it's easier to see you want just the opposite of what the other one's claiming, but now it's up to Paul to decide for himself and hold himself responsible for what's going on, and Paul he tells himself that that Claudie is funny stuff, kind of misshapen, never seen another woman with a top part like that, hollow long white with short legs like a boy's, and pink behind with round blubber. You'd never know what it's like to be tumbling with a Claudie, it'd make you like ashamed to be squeezing with her, little bitty pears and legs, but it's about Georges, the decision: if he leaves, Georges, things will turn bad with the animals and the farm, seeing our Vulva is sick and there'll be need of another darkie to come for the cows, and seeing you can't know if there's more big strong ones like him and agreeable to sleep in the glasshouse, on top of the extra work.

This Georges on the one hand he's straight, he's good-humored, he's honest for saying ahead it's to see a lady he goes out into the dark at night, in hail or drizzle even. On the other hand you have to grant that Georges brought us good times on the farm: since he got down off that bus and we put him in the glasshouse and since he said yes to taking on all the work he was given it's been easier to tick off the problems one by one and work out in your head what would be best to say or sell or plant.

Me, making no excuses for him, I can almost understand how Georges he let himself get taken in stupid, seeing the enticements there was: all them hussies they all scheme and work to destroy us, and we follow right behind, seeing they hold us in their spell, and I can bear witness even, for after dark Vulva when she was at home you always had to say no to her continual. So you have to understand how even some good workers, even dusky ones and advantageous to the farm, they fall for it, and I'm starting to see there's real need for a Georges to toil away on the farm till September.

"There's no affair over women that can part me and you, Georges," I finally decide loud and strong, "for what they're about is trying to smirch and destroy the good relation between the master and the farmhand, and him a foreigner on top of it."

And at that I knock back a brimmer and pour myself another plum. It bowls me over deep in my soul I can be so big, magnanimous like that and equitable, and I'm longing for my Georges to come home for me to hug him and squeeze him, a rare event for me, it comes into my head to land him a good clout by way of pardon and grant of amnesty, and it lifts me by the gut till I rise out of my chair: "Georges you old bugger, what a man," and I sit down in emotion and the joy of waiting.

"Whoa, hold on now," by good luck it comes back to me reasonable after that spell of foolishness and a full glass of plum drained off: "Have you thought yet about the criminal adultery affair?"

That's a business would bring the law down on you and a fine, and set the neighbors gossiping too, and it's complicity to let your Georges near that woman.

I've to tell him to end the affair right now, that's my resolution, and the carryings-on in full daylight that brought horror to your eyes and unworthy of a Georges deserving of his boss's esteem. The boss knows, he forgives, the boss he grants pardon and formal absolution, but only as long as Georges quits Claudie, and then we'll be grand on the farm, grand and united in a common purpose, the same for both, that's what I'm setting to say to my Georges, and that it's not worth destroying yourself over a woman that doesn't even have nice shapes and attractions to her body, and that's when Claudie appears; she's lovely naked, with a cover of earth in places; she says it's all roots and worms in that woods; she's lying in the bed; she catches me by the leg and hauls me and she yokes up; she's bare naked and shows, and she says: "Quick!" for Georges has to catch the train, so I say: "I'm touching your apples," but there's none, there's none at all, there's nothing but dirt, and then Georges asks: "Do you see her ball?" and shows me the big balloon she has in her belly, and I say: "Like Vulva," and then she laughs and in my bed I can see it's Vulva all wore out from having a wee one, and I bawl out, and right then the glass clinks and it lifts me out of my dream, and there's Georges leaning over me laughing: "Boss, you been drinking?" He's finished his day, Georges has.

"Hi boss," Georges he says, "Cheers!" and he sits down and tells how the animals is giving trouble, but it's really not serious, so if I'm sleepy he can tidy up and it will put no one out, and I say: "Maybe I'll just go to bed," for my head it's like a vise on me and it's not the right opportunity to take it up with him, about that woman.

24

On the meadow if you put yellow you can tell it's autumn, and the farm in red is lovely but not as nice as natural, seeing the talent for painting isn't the best of my make-up.

All the youngsters is inside, for outside the sky's thundery and it's Sunday as well so there's no school, and after the pork, the sauce, and the noodles, and the things you gorge yourself on with the Good Lord's blessing, Georges he said it'd be a grand idea to stay at the table all of us and take out the brushes and paint what we'd like or whatever comes into our heads. All the youngsters said yes, and I said we'll have to see, seeing that since I was a child, since before I grew up and got big and mature and broadened out, I've never taken up any paints, apart from the brown one on the gates. Georges he said: "You can do what you like, everyone's free," and then one of the youngsters said to do the house, and all the others set about it, and me and Georges as well.

The farm should never be round, it should never be side-on with the roof cock-eyed the way the youngsters do it, or with no doors: you have to be able to recognize it all with the right openings and all the cows at the windows so you can count them and be sure they're safe inside and well cared for, with their coats well groomed, eating their hay and happy there in their den.

The youngsters they can't understand, and even Georges he gives me a tough time for using red when now the gray's free for me to make the picture of my farm to my soul's content.

"In gray it's more like," says Georges to make me change. "A person could never recognize yours at all and it's like one that doesn't exist in the real," he comments to me trying to get mastery over my creation, so then I explain that's the way I see it and think of it, when I think of it: a nice wee farm in red colors with an orange roof, for that's the high spirits coming out, with the laughing inside and the joyful atmosphere you feel in the cow barn when they come back in and they're getting ready for the night, or maybe when they just want to spring outside for it's tearing at their hearts to get out to graze, and it's sparkling out of doors.

But Georges he feels no joy, he'd rather the roof weighed down stupid dull on gray walls and never see a soul nor a live chicken in the yard, and when you point out, he answers that's the way he feels, and if he drew someone it'd be no rooster but a lady, one it seems I've forgot, he'd swear, Georges. He draws me one with breasts and tits up front, so it's time for me to say: "It's Claudie maybe?" and Georges he looks me straight in the eyeballs and he says maybe so, or maybe we're missing another person, and he draws me another one bigger and fuller up front.

Right then it goes off in me: "And this one too, maybe, and that other one, and that other big lump, and all the ones you tumble on the ground in the woods," I bawl, and I scrawl red-painted hussies all over his drawing and wreck the whole harmony, one on the roof and another standing and another on her back in the cloud, and another planted in the sun. Georges he grabs away the paper but not so fast, for I'm holding on and it rips.

As soon as the yelling starts the youngsters are gone, they head off fast to the bedroom and Georges and me is left at one another eyeball to eyeball. Georges is angry, you can tell from the way the nostrils go in and out, but he says nothing, he's thinking quiet inside, and if he says more about a person that's not here I'll bring up about his that's not in the immediate either but is cluttering our heads.

Then Georges speaks. It's no lion's roar, he's in the grip of no anger, for he says, gentle like someone with no hate in him: "So you know about Claudie?"

He says "Claudie" so tender it falls like balm on the ears and it feels like a breeze passing, the breeze of Love I suppose, and it even sends a shiver, like seeing a newborn.

"Well," I answer, "let's say . . ." and I'm setting to recount the whole sight that met me, when Georges starts off like in a dream: "That Claudie, she's for real, she's real exceptional," and that starts the shiver again.

Seeing him all carried away like that I go: "For me, Georges, I tell you, Love's no snag, far from it, the snag's not the woman, it's the husband, due to the serious adultery."

139

And I explain for him like A plus B that the law will come after him, for about here it's not like in his home country, for here they jail folk that turns loose.

But there Georges he answers there's no problem from Charles: there's no cause to worry about him, but just let on he doesn't exist, like he was dead if I'd rather, and I can tell myself that that woman it's like she's single, seeing Georges he can assure me that from far back between Claudie and her Charles there's been no yoking, no feelings, and no bed.

"Yeah, but they're married," I object straight off.

They're maybe married, Georges says, but it makes no difference, it's like they wasn't, seeing Charles himself has another one he sticks to like she was his wife, and she's not Claudie, if I get what he's saying, and before that there was another, older and not so pretty, so if Claudie loves Georges her husband doesn't care, and he invites him in for a drink even when they meet, almost every evening.

"Charles he puts up with you going there?"

Oh indeed he does, and he extends him a warm welcome even, and he's even glad to see Georges for the entertainment, though he's not in the picture about the love affair and Georges doesn't sleep there, not to upset the norm, but it's just a matter of days and Georges and her they're working on it.

"Oh, so Charles doesn't know?" That consoles me deep down.

No, Georges he reckons, but at the same time he knows all about it, and for sure he guesses when Claudie goes out with Georges and they never come home till after dark looking all fulfilled and satisfied.

That's when I say I know where in the woods he tumbles her, but Georges doesn't seem to want me discussing further, so then I ask, just to be informed and up to date, if it's true Charles has other women too and Georges says they've made like a job contract between them that says unspoken that Claudie is to stay there for the farm and to help Charles, but not out of love at all, seeing he goes off visiting other females and squeezing them tight.

"But where does he find them?" I inquire, for about here it's no use keeping an eye out, seeing none ever comes near.

"You've only to look down at your feet to find them," Georges laughs, and then when he sees me gawping at him he explains further, for me to catch on: women, they're no problem, he says, you just need to be shaved clean for them to throw themselves at your feet, especial when you're like Charles and have a big farm to your name and no debts, no heirs, and a nice dark moustache on top of a big pot-belly.

It's the way he talks, Georges, and it inspires a wee notion in me that built like I am and with my own four strong walls I could have hundreds of women if I wasn't against, and it's like Georges is trying to convince me into grabbing a few to liven my evenings.

"It doesn't tempt me at all to have any others about here," I say straight out to cut him off, and that he shouldn't get worked up about it: "It would be possible, but I won't, one's enough for me already."

Oh, he knows that, Georges does, oh he knows very well how one's enough to brim over the cup and leaving no cause to be ever wanting any new ones, but Claudie has talked to him and explained how and why her Charles has others after her, and ones that aren't even young: there's never been harmony between Charles and her, never no love, none of the true, great, eternal love that's wrote with a capital L and grabs us in the head as much as by the crotch and all that. There's been only the look of it, a dull little spark that frizzled out in short order, just while they was getting married in church, for the next days when Claudie took a closer look at Charles she saw he wasn't the man of her dreams, and Charles at the same time he saw he didn't truly love this Claudie, and it was then the real misery set in on their farm, for twenty-two's far too young for getting married.

"Oh that's for sure," I agree back, me that was wise enough to bide my time.

Charles, Georges goes on, it didn't take him forever to bring in a girlfriend to substitute, but she wasn't right for him, so he tried others and took on a few, and all that time in place of the love of her dreams Claudie was left with her heart dangling and empty inside, and sad from the lack, but no one ever found out, for Charles he was discreet, and Claudie she was left wondering which of all the guys that went by far off would bring her satisfaction, so she waited and watched continual, night and day, till Georges turned up to take her into his arms.

"So I could have had Claudie, just for myself?" it flashes in my mind.

Georges he looks at me full on: well no doubt if I'd been with no Vulva and alone on the farm maybe I could, but who's to say, I'm maybe not the sort she appreciates, for she has her tastes, seeing it's only dark sorts she finds handsome, for she's wild about ones with a tan. Maybe that's why Claudie—Georges is just making a hypothesis here—never came this way and we never saw her around before they met on the road.

"She never came here, Claudie? Think again, Georges," I gave a laugh. "We've seen her about here frequent!"

And I tell how sometimes when Georges was away out in the fields or emptying the cistern or somewhere else, she would come by all friendly and stay half an hour or so, and I add up almost a dozen times at least or fifteen or sixteen on my fingers for him.

Maybe I'm exaggerating, I grant to myself, and maybe it was last year she came, or maybe earlier, to ask Vulva to hand over the stamps that earn you free gifts from the store, or maybe not, maybe it wasn't Claudie but some other hussy, or maybe I can't remember, or maybe I'm just saying for Georges so he doesn't go on fancying that just because you've salt and pepper in your beard and not the latest in work shirts there can't be one of them eyeing you like a handsome lover-boy.

Georges he's not persuaded, for he says: "Do you think so, do you think so?" with his little wide grin all cocksure and fearless, so I say to rile him and make him feel how in this part of the country he's a later comer than the rest of us, that it wasn't so far back Claudie took a fancy to me, to me Paul the boss, me of this farm, me the master of the herd and even nobler-looking then than now, with the head set straight on the collarbone and my hand firm on the stick, and I tried to act to show him, and back then we'd never heard of the Portugal country, and if we ever said "Georges" around here it was just to that hog we fattened up one year for the bacon.

There I make a pause to see if Georges wants to put in a word or a question, but there's never a sign out of him except his big grin, so I develop: Claudie back then was still good-looking.

"Like she is still," Georges puts in.

Well, near, I answer, but a lot younger then and with more attractions on her person. She would come into the yard all prettied up, and she visited a pile of times in spite of Vulva, and she came bothering Paul with her infatuation and distracting him off his duty, even though he had the work, plenty of animals, and no Georges nor no one else to help.

I let on I'm seeing her again, off looking at her like in a trance, and I go on: "Lovely, yes, like that, nice and young and lovely," like I'm far away. And then I specify for him not to think I'm tempted and want to steal Claudie for myself: "But not the sort I like, for she has pears too little and legs too," I say, remembering from the woods. And I add, to cover my tracks, Claudie has forgot about it for sure, for once a year at least she gets a new infatuation, and then I wait to see what kind of an answer Georges is setting to come up with.

Georges he says nothing.

"You're not angry over the drawing?" it crosses me intuitive.

It's true, the way you see it rolled on the ground with the big crack down from the sky through the walls and windows split into two mountains, you'd have to set it up to smooth it out and do it over, and you might as well take a new page and start fresh, so I suggest nice and helpful: "You'll do another one?"

"No," Georges he says: he says he feels no urge to, and it's a one-to-one talk he prefers, man to man, at our ease now the youngsters is gone, and you can tell he's off to confession just from the way he's leaning his head and crossing his two hands on the table.

Georges, he can talk about nothing but Claudie. He says right now she's the only thing he's carrying in his head, back of his eyes, in his ears, and especial he tastes with his mouth every minute of the day, and he carries her with him when he goes feeding the cows or milking, or when he goes out to the fencing, or taking his soup, or when he's up on the tractor, and when you think you see he has his mind on his work it's always Claudie he sees shining in his heart, though he does his work proper all the same and there's never an animal suffers due to it, Georges he swears.

He says she's like a flower, he says she's lovely like some woman you'd never feel free to dream of in your sleep but you see sometimes in a movie, but that's not true, after what I saw from the woods. She has things about her I could never guess, Georges describes, and when she laughs Georges sees it's written there they'll stay together always, for all the days God allows them. In all her spots she's soft, if I get what he means, and Georges he likes kissing and putting his head so much, and she has things hidden that's like little eggs, if I can picture, and other things Georges wouldn't like me to think though he couldn't stop me, but the best of all is she suits Georges so perfect he never had such sport before as since his Claudie fell for him, and she never wants to be parted from him again.

Georges he asks what I think about it, for he'd like my opinion, and I'm welcome to interrupt even if it's only to ask a question, but I don't know how it comes there's not a single notion in my head, just from trying so hard to make out all these tidbits on show.

Georges, all this business about Claudie he understands it's unsettling and muddling, and if it stirs up urges, as Georges guesses it does, that's just normal, due to the long absence of my own lady, my Vulva. He can only sympathize, Georges, and it upsets him and tortures his brain cells to be crazy in love like a donkey when Paul he's perishing from the lack, but she'll be back soon, or even if she never pulls through he'll surely find himself another to put in his bed, Georges has no fear.

Then he opens his big trap wide, and never even leaving me time to answer he gives a huge yawn and explains how on these Sundays with the rain there's nothing left worth a thing but the siesta, and he doesn't want to miss it, seeing on weekdays the boss talks with a big stick if there's even a hint of an urge to take off, Georges he laughs, and he says "See you later," and already you can see him outside chasing across the yard through the downpours.

Once Georges is out of the house it comes over me to reflect about the things that isn't for granted and others that aren't true at all: that first of all that Georges isn't right I drive him with a big stick, for I never have, even if I've felt tempted, but it was always in the fancy. Then Claudie and Georges telling Charles they're going out, and Charles allowing it, even if they come back after dark. And Charles with girls chasing him that aren't his own, and shouting it from the rooftops, or next best to Georges. Georges fancying Paul is longing for it, and saying it'll pass when Vulva's over the sickness. Vulva never coming back from the hospital and no effort made even to get her back. Claudie having pears for Georges but none for Paul. Paul free to grab at pears if he could have looked abroad off his farm and lowered himself to pick up all the ones hanging about, including Claudie herself, seeing Georges he caught her going along the road, and what difference to her if it's Georges or another male, or maybe even the other one's better, being as Georges isn't permanent in these parts.

Vulva doing the same one day and coming home with some brown joker to lead up the garden path. Paul deciding to take a girlfriend, another one than Vulva, for between both of a couple there's no love can last and penetrate, and not meeting Claudie but a different one, a prettier wee minx, and all the males over the countryside knowing Paul has Vulva on the farm and the other at his beck to tumble him on the ground and swoon after him bare naked, and Paul keeping with Vulva due to the farm, but never for the bedroom nor the nights: yes, but then nothing works right on account that Vulva never lifts a finger to go and rub down the animals and has never been able to set about working proper or hooking up the machines, and she's apt to wreck the whole thing, being she's unsuited to life, to life on a farm.

Vulva she stops you living the way you'd like, normal, the way you hear others say, for she's a millstone. Vulva's not made for this world and she wrecks the whole thing, in your dreams even.

Vulva, you could let on she's dead and act like she's in her coffin, but it'd make no difference, or maybe it'd just bring a tear, a sigh at closing down the lid, for all the same she was the wife you'd seen around here for ages, and now on top of it you're left to find another to replace her, and meantime there'll be no joy gotten from the farm.

25

All these nights I spend resting from my labors, from the farmer's sweaty toil, there's Claudie coming to mix in at all hours of the dark, waking me, tangling in my dreams and teasing till she has me wide awake and I'm never able to shut an eye again. It's sometimes Georges brings her, Georges out in the fields asking me to come and look, just to see the way in their simplest yoking they go about grappling and taking one another.

"No, that's enough!" I shout once the eyes come open, and the sleep's gone in a flash, and it's done for any rest and peace of the soul, for if it depends on itself it depends heavy on the body too. That's why at first light, when Georges hammers at the doorstep for someone to come and open from inside and let him in to his breakfast, I never answer his friendly greeting serene, and sometimes it seems like I'm tearing mad.

She comes for example when you're deep in your dream and she says she wants to milk when that's not allowed, and she straddles the animals and yokes with me. She gets into my bed too, like in the old marriage days, and I won't let her say "Yes," or she goes down my throat with her tongue that cuts sharp like that grass you sometimes suck in the fields. Or else it's with the youngsters she sleeps, and Georges brings her a naked dress that shows the dark places on the skin like real, and I see just the tips showing, the tips of the fruit, and I grab with my two hands, but Georges is off to saw wood for the fencing, and it wakens you.

There's no fathoming all the same how all day you labor long and crucify yourself with the zeal and toil of your work, and you never for one moment think of her out on the land nor again in the fields nor at the machines nor with the animals, and how you forget so total you never breathe a word of her to Georges, and even when Georges says "she" or "my sweetheart" or "my girl" you never answer and keep mum, but then sudden you think of her again the minute you lie down, and then she'll carry on like a wild thing the whole night.

It's not from me the notion hatches, I know that, it's not from my brain, it's out of this Georges the thoughts pour like pictures, and in his head it's so powerful and brimming over about his Claudie that the air's steeped in it everywhere and it colors all over the farm, even to the cows that can think of nothing but going to the bull, and even in broad daylight the young ones go blabbing to all comers their delinquent notions about how life gets conceived, and it's so mighty you can't work peaceful and quiet in the field any more without some of them turning up to ask where you put in the seed, into what office it goes, with the rest of them in a squad listening behind and laughing themselves silly.

"Now's not the time," I retort, "it's not decent," and I threaten them with my spade till they take off, but in every corner you catch them laughing at the filthy tales running through their heads about me and Vulva and what folks do in the nighttime, so the slaps rain on them at mealtimes when they go pinching one another and playing up or making sketches of their parts on the dinner-plates.

Georges he's of the opinion you should comment to them and put it all on the table just like they was equals and let them get up current with life and all the grand things that go on in it, for he reckons that at the boys' age it's unnatural never to know where you put the seed in nor where the fruit comes out, nor how you make the approach, nor for what outcome you grow.

"It's like everywhere," he suggests, "the grown-ups have to explain to the children," and he thinks it's a duty for the father to teach the children and be able to show how it's done, and if it's right or wrong or not, but if by chance the father appoints Georges in his place, Georges he's agreeable to looking after the education.

If Georges wants to handle the problem, me I won't say no, seeing he's at the root of all this trouble of having to explain why Adam's not made like Eve nor Eve like him, and Georges says he likes playing schoolmaster and he knows his pedagogy, especial when he has pupils like my brood that's dead keen to learn all about nature and the grand marvels of life, so now the urgent is to take your courage in hand and instruct them about growing and the instinct for propagating. But on the other hand I never say yes to the way Georges goes about it, proclaiming rampant and brazen the business of the flesh and the beast between his legs that grabs him evenings, and I'm more of a mind as a father to put the whole thing off long term till after the lads grow up proper men with hair on their chins and developed full, and I open up my thinking to Georges, but Georges he reckons he can find the right way to go about it, and he tells me about the bees swarming and such stupidness you can't see any relation to, except it's summer and they're raiding the flowers, and anyway when Georges talks about it I ask him to change the subject for I've no need of his explanations, seeing how many I have on my farm already.

It's that time after the cheese when the rain is holding us at its mercy and we're still dawdling on at the table fingering up the scatterings of crumbs, not that we're hungry but like they say to kill time for a while.

Georges, it's the time of day he prefers due to the black sky soaking outside, for he feels so at ease here with Paul, a glass at his right hand and at his left the good stuff that warms the gullet just right and lends a party feel, except it's Monday and with due respect to the master the tarps have to go on before nightfall, and Georges stretches out tall with his arms up to the sky, and right then the phone starts its ringing.

"Who can that be?" Georges wonders, for it's not often it rings, indeed it's never, and since from he was born he's been made to fancy the world spins just for him, he says maybe it's his brother looking for him, or his Mama, or maybe his little Claudie missing him from yesterday already.

"You likely want me to answer?" Georges he asks heading off to the dring with me still getting up after him behind.

"I'll get it Georges," I order with my voice swelling big from the chest, but his back carries on fast straight down the passage towards the ringing, and I bawl: "Let me get it Georges," for he's running quicker than my legs can carry, but just when Georges picks up I arrive and grab forcible out of his hand, and it's a surprise for Georges and the other person too, away there at the other end, so I make her the request to start over again, due to an incident around here that created a bar to hearing her.

The person explains she doesn't know to who she has the honor, so I illuminate her saying it's just me, Paul, the farmer that's master of the farm she maybe knows from going by, but the person says she doesn't, and then I explain the way to get to this part of the country coming from somewhere else, from the south or from other places. This person she really thinks the farm must be a sight worth seeing all right, but she regrets she has no time to take off for a holiday just like that, and she asks if maybe I'm the husband Paul, the one whose wife is sick, that had the tumor and had a surgery there and all goes with it, and I say yes that's right, and I squeeze my ear up tighter.

Then the person recommends listening attentive and asking questions after, if any come to mind, and I never answer, for my voice goes to bits in it.

The person talks away, but all the time she's palavering Georges is muttering and whispering excited to know who's on the line, till he gets me all muddled and I lash out with my one free hand, and the person off on the other end asks did I understand, and I say no, for there's some brute has come kicking up ructions here, and the person says she'll go over again, so this time I should concentrate and listen sharp: Vulva, if that's her real name, is free to return home to her family, for the chemical rays have had the hoped-for effect, but on a single condition, which is she stay sensible and quiet, keep to her bed a lot and sit a lot in the kitchen or in the chair in the living room, but there's to be no cooking of meals nor dishing up to the children, at which I say that'll put no great strain on her, for normal that's her activity in the farmhouse, always trying to read or yawning all day long, and I hear the person smiling and she asks if all the same there's a need to send a family helper till Vulva is better, so I answer we've a Georges here that does the house jobs, and anyway you could say we manage on our own, and we've not the slightest wish to see some other big lump at the kitchen stove.

"All right then," this person says, while Georges comes sniffing about at hearing his name and keeps prompting questions at me, so I explain low down it's nothing, it's about Vulva, and for him to hold his horses while I get on with the contact. The ear on the left says "Sir, maybe you have something to ask," but I reckon I don't, while in the one on the right Georges is saying: "Why not?" and in the left one it starts off again saying there's no time left, but if maybe I still want to know how she's doing, then of course.

"Who?" I ask.

The person answers she means Vulva, so I answer she's doing fine, and the individual says yes, well, we'll speak again and goodbye, and in case later I have some comments or questions here's her personal number, but anyway it has too many figures to remember and there's nothing around but the pencils the youngsters take to school.

The person sets down, and at the other end it goes blank, and Georges says nothing, for inward he's still riled, with never a whit of the cockiness left.

So: "Now to work," I go jovial at last, putting the top back on the cradle, and I ask the question straight if it's time to put the tarps on or not?

"What do you think, Georges?" I go all agreeable to demonstrate good humor and no resentment at picking up the talk again where the phone interrupted.

Georges he never answers.

"What do you think, Georges good buddy and Paul's right hand man," I go with an air of good nature, though of course I'm not that kind, but when Georges doesn't lift a finger it's a detriment for the fields, a detriment for the hay, a detriment for the woodlot and for all the beets still to come.

Georges he never even lets on he's heard and he heads for the yard, as if maybe he was off to the hens.

"We're going to have to set to work," I put in again before he goes out into the yard, "seeing when Vulva comes home there'll be twice the chores to do, what with pampering her with food for fear she pulls her disease on us again," and Georges he gives no more sign of going out but just chanced to hold back in the doorway to see the lovely sunlight falling outside with the bright spell.

"We're going to have to open the bedroom up again and put all proper in shape," I keep on to prime him with the notion that was mine in the first place, though Georges at the same time fancies it was his, of at last opening up Pa's room for Vulva to recruit in.

"We'll have to put our backs into it," I mutter to myself bending over the boots you jam on your feet when it's boggy in the fields, then Georges he turns a little that big mug of his that's holding a shine on it like it's lit up from sweat or surprise, turns his dark head a bit, and like it would hurt his lips to open his trap as required, he goes in a quivery voice, down low: "We'll have to rest her, that's for sure," and then he just spits and gathers up his jacket and goes to see in the yard if the sky's clear again outside.

26

Pa's room has been in shape since the word came, and now the shutters let in the sun it seems almost clean and bright like open country, with the bunches of flowers too that lack their pots that the youngsters will be responsible for, says Georges, from the day Vulvia comes in here, and it's true it's terrible nice and big, with white walls and shining chairs and furniture, clean of dust with never a flyspeck to be seen, so Vulva she'll forget total it was here Pa said goodbye to all and cursed Vulva for all eternity.

Georges he scolds every time I say the bedroom is Pa's. He says that's over and done, and now it's Vulvia's, till I point out he'd better take a look at the size of the big bed under the window, reaching so wide and covered so attractive with the new bedspread and the double eiderdowns all puffy that it might maybe be for Vulva to sleep in with a husband.

"Okay," Georges he says, but he forgets, and next day he corrects the same way after I call it Pa's: "Vulvia's, Paul," and he spends all the time he can rob from the hay or the feeding or the animals dreaming about things to do in there, if it might be possible to make it better in the room and more pretty than just four walls and two windows and a big double bed with expensive bedclothes, and two old chairs he painted white himself, and the mirror that's a present from Claudie and I don't like but we accepted anyway, for in our house we've always been polite.

On top of all, one fine day after dinner Georges he takes the notion to paint with a brush big round letters with flowers on the door to depict her name and surname, and he asks the boss about it, if he's agreed.

"Well," I say to Georges, "it's just it's a detriment to the overall harmony," but Georges he figures art can beautify a home, so already he's planning the colors and the designs.

Then one evening I'm checking up and passing by like by chance, and the door is all over rose bushes, and Georges is there at it using black for the lines and colors for filling in, but even in great big letters it's hard to read among the petals.

"What do you think, Paul?" Georges he asks, and I just go: "There's letters missing," and to explain I grab the brush, and then Georges isn't sure mine would fit in, but underneath I add *PAUL* in my own fist: too bad if the paint runs and goes all over the doorframe and the shoe-soles for it's the Portugal has to chase off after cloths to wipe with: it's the Portugal has to clean up and wipe and sweat and never make free to lift his head even to complain at the boss, who goes off calm to his field for a good smoke with his own that is happy out there munching his good grass, while back in the house the other's down like a dog scraping the mess off the ground.

When they're by themselves like that in the fields you get a pile of pleasure watching them out in the open, the way they love to feel the light of heaven on their coats like nature first wanted them in the world: with no rope, with no halter pulling on their necks but free in the breeze if the humor takes them to set off on a swinging trot, or maybe wander off to look behind a tree for juicier to munch, away from their stalls, so that with never a worry they forget altogether and live like they was Eve.

Georges he can never see what's important, he knows nothing about good simple pleasures, he just reckons the right thing for him is looking after females that foul the air and live real bad and go settling every detail of their homecoming when out in the open these ones is all aquiver, wandering over the grass, fulminating at the flies with their long tails and lowing natural, miles prettier and more attractive than the other one with her grunting.

I go among them, through the heads and horns, and they smell me, they recognize me by ear and they turn to me when I call, seeing it's always good times when I come, it's always a treat I bring, and they follow me quiet, they push at my sleeve for salt, and I feel in my left pocket if there's something to give, and in the right pocket, and they wait patient, and even if their Paul finds nothing to offer they never complain and keep on looking, almost with a smile if you think about it.

"What do you think, Paul?" he said, Georges.

And me I answered: "There's letters missing," and I wrote *PAUL* on the door in big black thick lines that rained splashes over the rest and splattered his rubbishy roses to show again what Paul wants and what's the real stuff he's made of, and Georges he stood there gawp-mouthed like a tree-stump and catching on who's the decider on this farm.

Georges, he always comes devious, mixing his fork into affairs and dragging unpleasantness into the daylight, and it would real embarrass if you didn't know it's just Georges and from your personal point of view it's not important what he rakes up.

"When's she coming home?" Georges he asks again when we're chatting about Vulva, regarding that person at the end of the phone and the information she gave.

"When's she coming?" like he fancies maybe I can guess, till he makes me cough up I've no notion, for the person at the other end on the phone never answered that.

"But," Georges keeps on, "for sure you must have thought of asking?"

Well natural I held it a while in my head, natural one minute I tried to say they shouldn't send her back to us too soon due to the peaceful impressions she leaves us from being away, and I don't know how, but somehow it got lost going along.

"But how do we know when the day comes we have to go and fetch her from her room?" he frets, Georges, for he's imagining it'll give a chance to have his sport strolling round town when there's things need to be done back here, and now more than ever, since Georges keeps going off all the time to check in the bedroom if it's all clean and in shape.

"Never you worry," I console, "we just have to watch for the bus that goes past in the day, and the youngsters they'll do their job and shout right off if by chance it's bringing Vulva back to us."

Georges he doesn't like me saying: "We just have to watch," he thinks, with respect it's almost a lack of consideration for the mistress of the farm, for maybe coming out of the hospice like that she's too weak to travel all alone on the bus.

"Well then they'll have to keep her if she's still feeling weak, for there's a shortage of room about here for them that doesn't stick to their post," I say short, but Georges keeps watching out every day from far, and when the bus comes in sight he drops the shaft and runs for the stop yelling: "She's here, Vulvia's here," with the young ones skipping after, and when it starts up the road again the youngsters run after the gases, and the farmhand comes back to pick up the tool at the spot he left off.

One thing Georges has hard to imagine is that Vulva is cured and already she's up on her feet, for according to his calculations after all the months of medicating he'd have wagered Vulvia's time had come for the priest and her quarters in a box under the sod.

"You understand, Paul," he demonstrates, "with that big ball in her belly shoving her gut out of shape, it was barring a miracle Vulvia never had a chance of not dying," and he wonders what kind of a trick they used to cut out the canker without her expiring at the same time.

Them isn't things Georges should have let out normal, them is thoughts and ideas that stays shut up in your head due to the glum they generate and because it's not right, even if you know, to talk about the end ahead of time, but now Georges can show it, now it's okay for him to tell how hard it was to act like he thought

Vulvia would ever come home and put on high spirits and act the mainstay of the farm, but now Georges can admit how it tortured him mental-wise to be the only one seeing and yet be powerless to warn, and rising every morning first thing Georges would think that poor Vulvia was a goner, but thank God by good luck Georges was mistook, at least this time, though it sometimes happens doctors make mistakes too.

So says Georges, but me I'm total different inside: I knew right from the start our old girl would recover back due to the sturdy constitution that has always kept her on her feet, even in the worst conjugal dust-ups, and that Vulva she was well able to face out the storm and strong enough to survive hurricanes too, the kind of critter you can never finish off for it wears you down. And that time here on the farm, long before Georges ever set foot on it, after the fridge broke down, after that meat gave us the big stomach upset, Vulva never felt a thing in her bacon and ate by herself alone at the table that night with a smile all over her mug just like we was all there.

Yeah, says Georges, but that proves nothing: him too when he was a youngster he'd sometimes get the colic, but now his gut digests anything at all with no problem, like sardines: Georges he can go on forever rambling about himself that way if you never stop him, if you never call to his attention time's passing and there's a field still to be finished, or other more important things calling for more sweat than jawing, and of greater profit to a farmhand if he's still worth his hire.

27

The kitchen when I get there is empty with no young ones at the cooking, likely they're out at the hens, gathering eggs out of the straw, but it's not like normal, so I poke about the stove and I find every saucepan cold and nothing steaming and nothing to show it's near time for the evening meal.

Georges, he must have some dodge holding him up, or else he's skulking in some corner on account of me painting in the letters, or maybe Claudie's tumbling him in the forest, so maybe I'd better eat a heel of bread, seeing the two of them in a grapple can last a long time.

The bread, you'd figure it's not in its place, not in the corner of the sideboard.

One thing strikes your ear and that you notice right off is the quiet through the house, an unusual quiet that normal you never hear in the farmhouse due to the young ones always filling the air with their shrieks. You can hear even the hens scratching after worms and cackling, them that's always quiet out of terror at the danger of being ridden on, and away far there's a car goes by on the road, and maybe another, and the clock going tick-tock inside your head that you never notice for the day goes by too quick, and the flies crazy against the window in their electric bouncing.

The gruyere, there's none in the fridge nor none nowhere, and under the cheese cover it's empty as my belly.

Georges has quit the farm it flashes through my head, Georges has run away off the farm due to the painting, and he took food for his supper, the robber, and never saying a goodbye to a soul he set off back down South, and at that a tearing fury comes over me and I slam my fist into the wall, when right away I hear Georges' voice in the passage saying real low: "Come quick," in a quivery little whisper, and he comes into the kitchen.

"Paul . . ." he says, but I give him no time to go on, for I bawl: "Where's the cheese, and where did you put the bread, you rob- ber?" shoving him up against the wall and shaking the bread-bin by the lid with nothing but crumbs pouring out like dust.

Georges, he doesn't know what to answer, he just asks me to let go for there's a thing he has to say, but first I want to know what he's done with the cheese, and Georges he informs me right off the cheese is in the bedroom, along with the gruyere and the bread.

"But why are you taking the cheese into my bedroom?" I ask Georges, me all surprised but calmed down now, "that's no place to be eating," I say to him too, and Georges laughs with his eyes all shiny, he says it's not in mine but in Vulvia's. He says: "Come and see," and I follow along, though this kind of thing sends me crazy on top of the raging famine I have in my gut.

"And God only knows where them vermin is," I sound off again, though we're there already, and Georges says: "They're with . . . " but I've no time to ask what they're with when Georges has opened the door already and shoved me through and up to the bed, and who's lying there now but Vulva.

"There," he says, Georges, and I never say a thing, and nor does Vulva.

"Well . . ." I go at last, and Georges he says: "The bus set her down on the road when you was at the cows," and all excited he tells me the story, and me I stand staring straight at Vulva, and she back at me with her eyes sunk down hollow.

Vulva? Can that be our Vulva in there?

All you can see is a head sticking out of the bed, pale and thin and red, with eyes like at the bottom of funnels and the hair now a paler shade and long to the shoulders.

"She's back, Vulva's back," it chats in my head, "it's your lump of a Vulva, the big lump of a wife off your farm," and it bothers me at the same time that some moments the whole face turns into another woman's and I can see no Vulva no more, just some stranger woman, and I look away till the real one comes back.

The youngsters is struck dumb, they're standing bunched up in a corner against the wall; there's one looks through the window and another sits on the sill. They're watching from distant, and when Georges waves them closer to say hi to their Ma and give her a peck there's not one steps up, and Georges asks two times five times till he loses patience for real and gives a big clap with his two hands and the whole of the youngsters spurts outside like scared cats.

Then the lady stretches out an arm that's real thin and she nibbles a piece of cheese.

"You see," he whispers, Georges, "I brought the bread and the cheese, for Vulvia's starving coming off the bus and the doctors instructed she should eat a lot any time she liked."

"Well, let her stuff herself on them," I go to myself, "as long as she leaves a decent slice," but my gut's sucking at me, watching her chewing away like a she-ogre.

"Want a piece?" he offers, Georges, for he can always guess what you're thinking, but I answer no out of pride and discomfort at sharing with her, and seeing I'm not used to eating bread on the sheets.

"Whatever you like Paul," Georges tells me, and sitting down right on the bedspread he cuts himself a big thick slice and: "Cheers," for I hadn't noticed he has a bottle on the floor, and all the while I'm squying at it he explains obliging it was the doctor wrote in his epistle she's supposed to drink a lot of red to fortify up the corpuscles, but since Vulva's got no thirst for it he Georges is setting the example for the support and to comfort her.

But then I let on I'm surprised at what epistle's he talking about, and Georges says he'll explain, but first if I want to see, here's the document, and he pulls a page all crumpled out of his pocket, and I let on I'm reading through.

At the top there's printed "Hospital," and a few other lines as well, and then there's written "Dear Sir," and at the bottom it's signed with a black squiggle you'd take for a scratching-out, and I've no heart to go into it.

"Georges," how can I handle it? "I'm not real inclined for reading right now. When there's a little more peace and quiet," I say, rolling the page up in my pocket and making like I'm intending to read it somewhere else when there's time, and by good fortune Georges can't hold back from telling the whole thing ahead: it comes direct from the head man of the hospital, Georges tells me soft and quiet in my ear, for she's fragile mental-wise, with instructions written on what she has to eat, how much she has to sleep, how long she has to go walking, and what way to behave and how long her convalescence on the farm should last.

Convalescence? Now that's a surprise.

"Yes," he says, Georges, for even she's not as sick any more it's not certain she's cured, and for her to get back into shape, well, she still needs to be watched to stop her relapsing on us before we can get her back into top form.

"So they didn't cure her away in that place?" I say low down for fear Vulva might hear, but she sneaks a glance sideways like she catches all's being said.

"But for sure they've fixed her up good," Georges proclaims loud and strong," it's just she still feels real weak due to the chemicals in her system. Isn't that so?" he asks, and she goes "Yes," and then there's a silence closes down.

It puts you out to be standing next to your wife with the farmhand sitting on the bed and you not knowing how to go about telling her a friendly word, nor able to let her know in spite of all was said there's no complaint at her lying there in bed or being back home, no objection as long as she behaves like expected.

Georges he lets the hush lie heavy on us a while, and then he explains Vulva's tired out, and Vulva she goes yes with her head, and she has to pay attention to eating, and Vulva shows him the cheese she's kept a tight hold of but she's having it hard to finish, I can see that a mile off for I've no need of anyone to interpret Vulva for me, seeing as even operated on, even total changed, I know what she's feeling better than she does herself.

"Now," Georges gets up sudden, "the spouses have to chat together alone," and he heads for the door, and when I follow he advises me: "Just stay a while, Vulva's desiring to have her Paul all to herself for sure."

He says "desiring" with a wink, like he was talking about Claudie, and he pushes the door, and the two of us is left by ourselves, me and Vulva, like in the early days, except it's not the marriage bedroom and I've no notion what to do with a Vulva, and Vulva herself seems like a different woman with hair of a different sort and a face with changed looks.

Okay, I say to myself, if this Vulva has something to tell me, let her speak.

But Vulva brings nothing out clear, just a spare little belch, and then she looks down at her two pale hands, and after three minutes long she shuts her eyes and dozes, or at least I suppose so, for she never opens them and never shifts.

"Well then, I'll be going, Vulva, I'm off outside and I'll come back later," I say then to inform I'm going too, and then I put in for her not to fancy she's left alone and come over scared: "I won't be long," and I leave, closing the door proper behind me.

In the kitchen Georges is sitting, and it's no surprise there's plum in his glass already: from the day he arrived Georges has fit in real good, and it's just as well he's not staying year-long, for the stock of bottles I have would never quench his gullet.

I sit down at the table with him, and the two of us look one another frank in the eye: "What do you reckon?" I say to Georges.

Georges he stares down into his glass.

"I hope she'll start back on the farm working for us," I go to him gloomy.

"Of course she will," says Georges, "just leave her time to get better and into stronger form."

There's a gap of silence while we take a swig, and then Georges he starts yarning again, telling about Vulva and how she arrived: all overjoyed at the homecoming, he near forgot I wasn't there at the bus-stop and missed the moment, so incredible memorable, when Vulva in her best set her foot down off the bus, and then when I raise no objection he starts off, Georges: though like other days Georges he heard the bus coming far off down the road and the young ones shouting "It's the bus!" and running off to the stop already. But Georges he thought to himself: "It's not even worth the trouble going," and: "It's no use hurrying," when he heard the youngsters yelling to come quick for Vulva was there on the bus. Georges he thought to himself that them young ones tells lies all the time and afterward when you arrive in a sweat and out of breath there's no one getting out and the driver looks down angry asking if Georges is going to get in, and Georges he says no and the driver puts on a crabbed mug and grumbles he doesn't stop for nothing nor for brown ones that put the timetable in arrears, and he starts off, and Georges he breathes in the pollution gases with all the people squying down at him from up in the windows.

So this day, says Georges, this very day today of Vulvia's arrival, he takes his own sweet time getting there, making no haste to see her, and when the youngsters yell out: "Vulva's on the bus! Vulva's on the bus!" he just looks off over the land mechanical, never budging, sure no one was getting off.

The bus it stopped at the halt like normal, with the same big driver, and Georges is starting back at his work when sudden he thinks: hold on, the bus is taking its time this evening, and then he notices the door's opening like there's someone getting on or off, with all the young ones in a festoon along the roadside waiting for something.

It was that minute he caught on, Georges he says, that this was the very day Vulvia was coming back to us on the farm.

So he ran to the stop, and all the while he was running you could see someone standing up in the bus windows, something like white gauze, and then more time went, and a narrow stripe came into the doorway, and then there was a person getting off, like a little child on Sunday with some white thing and a dress, very slow, and from far he still doubted it was Vulvia for sure, or maybe it was some stranger lady that got off by mistake.

"You noticed that too?" I say, with respect to the stranger lady.

"Yes I did," says Georges.

The youngsters they stepped forward at the same time as her, but keeping their distance out of awe, and Georges came to meet her while the bus took off, and bit by bit he was looking and checking it was Vulvia coming for true, only with her body lighter and no luggage, just a wee bag under one shoulder.

Just when Georges got close, Vulvia she stopped to lift her head that she'd kept hanging down all the time, and she looked at him, and Georges caught on that Vulvia was saying hi with her eyelids, so he said hi back to her with his best big broad smile for reassurance, for Georges he could see how she was shaking and it was hard for her to walk, so he said: "I'll carry you," and he lifted her in his arms and he carried her real quick into the bedroom, for Georges is sure if he hadn't Vulvia would have stumbled, like Christ on his mountain.

"Yes," I say, for this gives me worry, "so she can't keep up on her legs?"

It's even more serious than I thought.

"Wait for the rest," he says, Georges.

When Vulvia she sees Georges isn't taking her into our bedroom, she comes over uneasy and asks for the first time since the bus: "Where are we going?" and she says "I'm thirsty," to which Georges answers now she has a room of her own, Vulvia's very own, and there's something in the kitchen for her little tummy.

"For her little tummy?" I laugh, to show how ridiculous, but Georges pays no attention or else doesn't catch what I'm thinking, and he carries on with his story.

Once they get into the bedroom—and this is what Georges wants to come to—if I could just have seen her face looking at the furniture and the chairs and the big broad bed Georges laid her in right off and put her under the covers.

"Hmm," I go, just to express my displeasure on account of the name on the door.

"And now," asks Georges, "what's she doing, is she sleeping?"

"Well, I suppose so," I answer, "she says she wants a little peace and quiet," telling him a wee lie, and Georges he's still looking real relieved.

Georges he found Vulva altered in her looks, and in spite of the serious illness he found her fresher, but I don't agree, I say, for there's furrows on her face, and Georges says it's due to the starvation, but her cheeks will fill in from the eggs and the cheese and good farm food, and I point out too her hair has gone all funny, and then Georges he has a good laugh that's too loud for his gullet and hurts his gut, so I have to wait, and when at last he's finished he explains it's not her real hair but false ones made of plastic for the interval till the real hair comes out again.

"Well I can't see what's so funny," and I feel a grudge rising in me, and Georges decides to stoke up the fire, and on top of it all Claudie comes bursting in like it was her own place.

"Good evening gentlemen," she shouts screeching like ten old biddies, and Georges goes: "Sweetheart!" and he licks her with his tongue so I have to look away, and then Georges tells her Vulvia's back in the bedroom.

"So she's here?" and she looks at me like she'd no trust in her man, but I never trouble to answer.

"Are you coming out for a while?" she goes cloying up to Georges.

"Well," says Georges, and it's easy to see he's riled, "we've not eaten yet, nor Vulvia neither, to get her back on her feet," and he goes sneaking a look down deep in the drawer, and then he answers some other day or maybe tomorrow, and that sends Claudie on her way all upset, and I tell myself maybe sometimes Georges isn't a bad sort after all.

28

It's Vulva's first day, so I'm willing, like Georges says, for her to get the best honey and good butter and good hand-ground coffee brought to her in bed to lift her morale and her appetite, for it's not big, and restore her complexion pink and glowing like it was.

It's her first sunrise on the farm since Vulva took her sickness and we sent for the doctor that put her into his hospital, and she'll not be rising early, Georges he said that wouldn't be good, so she'll get up when she likes, and after five on the wrist there's not a sound in the room yet.

For a little moment I go across and I lay my head to the doorframe all the while Georges is washing the table, while Georges is tidying up before we go out, and I keep real quiet, but there's nothing you can make out except maybe like a breeze coming in little waves, but then Georges comes and interrupts my observation: "What's up?" he asks. "Is she sleeping?"

And me I let on like I know: "You'd fancy she's saying things," I go mysterious, "and it's moving inside," but when I make to push open the door to take a look Georges stops me sharp by the shoulder and says Vulvia is dozing from the fatigue, and if we go in to look it's dangerous for her peace and quiet due to jerking her out of her dreams; then Georges goes back, for he still has the plates and the saucepan and the bowls to rinse before the sun's up, and seeing he fancies I'm going too I stay put and keep on spying.

When you put your ear up you can still hear that breeze and the washing of the little waves that sometimes whisper gentler on purpose to make you lose the rhythm, and the silence lasting so long makes you fancy Vulva's not alive still, for the sighing has stopped. And bit by bit with the waves coming and the whisper like of a breeze, it murmurs inside me at the same time too that in all them nights-long of marriage Paul never took the notion to turn on a light to see what Vulva looks like with her eyes shut and maybe the drool running down her cheek.

I push the wood with never a creak.

In the kitchen Georges is still stuck at the dishes with his two hands in the sink rubbing the bottom of the plates, for he often says it upsets him if there's butter left stuck, for it's not clean, and he likes it to be shining like the first day you used it, and usual I don't allow, I say to leave the small ones soaking in the big, for it's time to be outside, and I push him out, but today I have to see, so I slip in with never a creak.

Vulva, she's sleeping.

In the room it's almost too much, the sound swelling, like maybe it was the seaside, the way you imagine the waves playing their tune under the gulls. Maybe Vulva has a stoppage in the nose, or maybe she has a bad cold? Maybe the hospital air gave her a chill due to the want of blankets and the lack of comforters, so now she's caught a problem in the bronchials.

I listen a while to her breathing under the sheet, turned to the wall. I can tell it's her just at a quick glimpse, Vulva, she's lying straight out grunting and turned to the wall and she'll be snoozing till the morrow with no notion of what's going on and no clue about the potatoes nor the alfalfa nor what's happening with the animals—all the things that jockey about inside my skull.

I go close, I go all soft and precautious with my soles, and as I move noiseless Vulva in her sleep goes Euuugh . . . errghh . . . with her mouth, and the bed heaves up and the covers is thrown back showing Vulva asleep going Grmml grmml and sighing and making Mmm-mmm with her lips, like out of hunger or a lack of spittle.

Without me making another move Vulva quiets down sudden.

Now she's shifted, like on purpose for you to see what she's like asleep, to let you look on at your leisure.

The first big scare is the bare white of the naked head, and the hollows too, for it's not a nice pleasant thing to look at, and of course I remember from last night Georges laughing about the hair, but all the same it deals you a shock, a head with no hair and nothing to hide the naked skull. It's not the same face as before, skinny the way it is, and you fancy it looks like there's maybe a heap of things going on back of it, that maybe it's full of scheming, and maybe you'd like to be sure, but there's not a thing you can do. There's just the lips puffed out with the breathing, moving with a rise and fall, and the cheeks all hollow and empty, far hollower than usual, for the hospital leaves a person skinny.

174

It's carrying on a bit monotonous, this sound out of Vulva, and there's nothing happening anyway and it's time to get going in case Georges comes, for then he'll blame me if Vulva dies or if she relapses back into the sickness. But quick, there's still just that hair you want to run your hand through due to the way it crackles, the way it's good sport to ruffle between your fingers and it gives off like an electric, but quick, put it back where it was on the table, and off I go to the door. Before I close it, I don't know why, I put my lips to my fingers like saying a goodbye on the way out, and then I go to see what Georges is holding us up with.

Georges he's still at the washing and drying.

"Just look at that," he goes all proud of himself, "you can almost see your face shining in it," and it reminds you of TV, when the lady looks at her reflection in the plate, and Georges too, for he says it's like in the ad.

"And what about work, is that like on TV too?" I go light-hearted, just to make fun, but at the same time pushing strong. Georges he laughs, and there we are outside, with the sun headed up already.

Georges he steps out a bit into the yard in the cool and silence of morning, and now I know him I can tell ahead of time he's setting to preach more of his blather at me, and I don't have to wait long before he starts at his sermonizing: "How are you going to act with Vulvia, when she wakes up?" he asks me straight out.

"Well, I'll say hi to her," I answer, for you can never catch on to what he means.

"But how?" he asks, and I don't know, I've no notion how to say what it'll be like, so I just go: "Hi Vulva, with a smile if possible," and lo and behold he finds that's a good answer.

Georges, he wants me to learn the right way to chat and behave at a patient's bedside. He says for him there's no problem, for he learned in school, but in my case he's afraid it might be hard for me to find the right attitude appropriate for Vulva.

"You mustn't treat sick people rough," Georges he preaches, "you have to give them all their peace and quiet," and he carries on all the while we're hitching up the trailer, and once he's up on the tractor he shows the right way to chat to people in bad health that has something gone off track in their physical makeup: you must never bawl nor shout loud the way maybe you'd do normal, you must never yell at them, never talk this way, like he is right now, or with the loud voice he sometimes has evenings, but it's rare, when after the wine you start saying what comes into your head and arguing debates, Georges he starts roaring: "So, Vulvia, was that a good sleep you had?" and: "Hi Vulvia, is everything okay?" so it shakes the whole barn, and with big belly-laughs after, and even me that's not hard of hearing and solid in the eardrums I ask Georges to clam down his trap and give me some peace and quiet for my skull.

"You see," says Georges, "the effect it gives to Vulvia speaking things loud at her?"

Well of course I catch on if I go all thundering it'll give her a headache, Vulva, but if I talk low with a little soft voice instead, like you put on when there's a cow calving, or a gentle caressing one like when the calf's looking for the place to suck, then Vulva she'll fancy she's gone to heaven with the angels lulling her with their hymns.

Georges he's glad I catch on. He says I've made progress.

"Progress? At what?" I ask, and Georges he squys at me, he shows me broad the whites of his teeth, and he pronounces: "Progress, Paul, in the conduct of your life," all solemn like he took himself for the priest at his sermon, and that leaves me driven to answer like a half-wit: "Maybe we should go and see if she's moving?" so Georges has to trouble to explain over again that Vulva must keep lying down and sleeping as much as she wants, and he never notices I'm laughing when I start up the engine.

We turn along the rows of lime-trees, and it's me steering, for Georges isn't used to this farm machinery, and all the same I don't believe he knows how, like he says, and anyway I like driving straight across the land any old way, steering dead over the fields across rocks and grass.

Georges says there's one thing I don't do right and to be frank I do wrong, and that's going like I do into the bedroom in my boots and milking coat: that gives her a jolt, Vulva, it sheers the nose off her getting the stink of the animals, or maybe worse, right under her nostrils that way, and as well, since we're on the subject, Georges figures it doesn't always smell like roses if you wear the same shirt all the time, and then I put her into second, for that's near effective at covering it all, and Georges shuts up and bounces about, for we've cut across.

We stop in the meadow where there's toil and sweat in store, and I issue Georges his instructions for the fencing, plus the tools from the trailer, and we go at it silent, for contrary to his habit he keeps his trap tight and says hardly a word except "Hand me the wire," or "Yeah, I'm holding it," and that's all's needed when a pair is working hard together harmonious on the job.

It's the way I like to work: two solid mates, two heads that know how to put their backs in and never open their traps more than's needed, misplacing no questions about meals or the Bible or a swallow flying by or a cloud in the sky, nothing outside the sphere of the cows and the property of the farm. It's what I want on my land, and there's no farmhand here for the summer that's going to dictate the way to talk or please or behave or what to wear on the farm you're master of, for God's sake.

That's what's churning inside my head all the time I'm pounding on the stake with the sledgehammer, and so hard that Georges he suspects for sure it's for him, so he stoops over and works silent, like in the early days before he took on himself to stick his nose into my dirt.

"Holy shit," I say out strong, for now I'm really stewing and worked up into a state the likes of which even Georges himself hasn't put me in for a long time.

"Holy shit," I go again, and Georges doesn't dare to inquire, he just peeks in little doses, like he was afraid I'd chop him with the axe I'm heaving, and on purpose I take a squy at him to let him know it's in my mind.

In the end the sweat's dripping and the arms is dragging heavy, so I'm forced to stop a minute for it to ease off, and when Georges sees I'm looking away over the land and holding my side he says low down like maybe it was risky, timid like he used to be to his boss in the early days: "Maybe we could take a break?" Then I notice Georges he's all red in the face and dripping from the forehead too, with dark rings in the armpits, and likely the same parched gullet as well, but I never brought the bottle nor the flask.

"What about a drop of the hard stuff?" I go to him short, and when Georges all happy goes "yes" I say there's none left, and seeing our Georges all flattened crushed and gloomy gives me back my good humor and lets me know Georges isn't that massive strong after all and easy to tame, so I get back a bit of the taste and possibility of chatting.

"We never brought the strong stuff," I say short, and I fill in the picture, "and there's no juice in the can." So then Georges figures the best is to go back to the farmhouse, especial, he says in his low voice, that Vulva has to eat and by now the poor thing must be half starved.

It's true with this talk of smells and work-shirts we never gave much thought about the Vulva situation any more, for we're not used to her being present again continuous, and Georges he's right to remember about feeding her, indeed it's imperious, being as on her own she can't even rise out of bed.

Then I issue the instruction: Georges he's to stay here in the field when I go to Vulva and bring something back for him to wet his gullet, but of course Georges he protests that hanging about here with no fluid the sun's giving him heatstroke and I say: "Okay then," but I let on it's a nuisance, and on the way back I mutter on purpose: "Like a baby on the farm!"

So Georges he does no sermonizing on our way to eat nor any of the things he likes to dish out otherwise, and he never opens his mouth till we stop in front of the barn, but when he jumps down on his feet he goes: "We'll make her an omelet and bread and butter, and coffee just the way she likes it," but I tone him down to stop him rushing ahead on his own, and it's the two of us going to feed Vulva together.

When we get to the kitchen we're floored: what do we see but Vulva sitting at the table all dressed and wigged, and as well Claudie smoking the place out, and no sign of the young ones that for sure is off playing in the woods. There's the coffee pot too beside the cups and the honey, I notice to myself, and you can see Vulva has helped herself to her portion of meat already.

"You're here, Claudie?" he asks, Georges, like he's blind, and Claudie she tells how Vulva was out of the bedroom already when she came, and helped her with the coffee and breakfast things, for by ten in the morning it's time for a bite.

"Isn't that so?" she goes, and Vulva answers yes.

Georges he's not sure Vulva has eaten enough, he keeps on asking what she'd like, maybe some bread, or maybe she'd like to try the omelet he makes that's fantastic, and he tells her the recipe, plain or with nice herbs, but seeing we haven't got any, a plain one; he keeps on and on: "Wouldn't you like some?" till I'm famished in my gut and Claudie scolds it's enough, for poor Vulva just wants a little peace and quiet to rest. Georges stops his fussing and stays leaned against the cupboard, and we look at Vulva, the three of us, and she stares straight ahead at the butter.

"Is it hot out?" Claudie asks, making the effort for everything to be like normal.

"Yes," we answer, me and Georges together, and then Georges says with respect to the coffee pot: "Was it good at least?"

It's a question pointed straight at Vulva, but it's Claudie takes it, for the other's kind of sleeping, meaning she seems away far and hears nothing, so Claudie tells how she poured it into the filter herself.

"Well, that's okay then," goes Georges, and all the noise dies off again.

Vulva she has a fly walking on her arm and it goes up her neck twice and climbs down her chest and up and down again, and Vulva of course never feels a thing through the dress with the pattern, and maybe the fly's getting its kicks tripping round the flowers, once round, once in, maybe once across, and I'm like off in the moon with my eyes on the chest that's not so full any more I guess nor too inflated in volume, and I go the same way, the fly down, the fly up, the fly in the valley, till Vulva's eyes lift up and reach into mine.

Vulva she still has the flat eyes, you'd say like there was a veil across them.

At first it gives you like a shock to see Vulva can move about, that Vulva can show she's reflecting and can turn her eyes on her farmer husband, and it's almost a bit scary too to come against blanks like that, so right off I change directions out of awkwardness.

The fly's walking on Georges' forehead, and he puts his hand to it. Claudie says she's off, and that reminds me I lingered a long while on the dress paying no attention to what was being said, with Vulva off in the moon.

The fly comes back on the forehead, cheek, eyes, and nostrils, so you'd fancy it really likes Georges due to his sweat or maybe for other reasons, and then onto Claudie who he's arranging to meet, and then onto me, and then I shake up my ideas and say out: "Time to get going, Georges."

The three of us stand up to leave, me, Claudie, and her Georges, and when we get out into the yard Georges calls again to Vulvia she should rest sensible in bed till mealtime, and from inside the kitchen it comes back to him "Thank you."

29

What we're setting to have on the farm is a grand party for Vulva coming home, and for once Paul himself was the one inspired.

Georges says he helped all the same when he suggested we could put lanterns up in the leaves, set out chairs, and drink to Vulva's health, but I rectify he never thought up a real party with lanterns, red wine, sausages with cabbage and garlic, and things we like but normal never get to eat, for it's what you eat and slake your thirst on makes a party, we're agreed on that a hundred percent.

There was the problem of who to invite for Vulva: Georges he said if we brought in five or six of the neighbor sorts we have around here she'd like that, including Claudie, her husband Charles and Jean-Robert and Martial and everyone that's had a brush against the farm, but me I reckon intimate makes the best atmosphere, and already if all the young ones is going to eat it adds up to a big heap of food.

All the same, it's not so easy to know if she's agreed, Vulva. There's no telling what she wants, for we never discuss with her: we're aiming to surprise her, and the way Georges he pictures is when she sees the yard all prettied up with the lights in the leaves she'll let out a cry of joy and be real content she's back with us on the farm.

Her happiness for now she's kept it for herself, and she never turns out, she sticks to her bedroom and when you knock she answers she's sleeping, or she gives no answer at all, and whenever you call her to round up a hen or for the milking, or to lend a hand, she says she's resting out of fatigue, and you have to believe her, for Georges he says she's entitled, due to the belly.

It's often evening when she comes out for the soup. She comes silent to the table, and sits, and then the youngsters eat almost proper, sticking their noses in their plates. Georges, he's the only one talks to her and is able to find things to say. He tells the day over to her and what we did at the fencing, and he explains about the cows for her, and Vulva goes hmm . . . hmm . . . or uh-huh, but she says nothing on her own, maybe it'd be too hard on her gut.

Sometimes I try chatting to set her at ease, so she feels good and at home here in my house, and I say the likes of: "Did you see that cheese?" or: "This bacon's good," never asking any questions straight and avoiding any jolt to the system, but there's seldom an answer except hmms and uh-uhs like for Georges, so there's never a useful thing comes out of her.

Anyway it's no surprise Vulva's stubborn as a carp, it's the same as ever, like it always was before, for it's in her nature to be witless and unsocial, and me, I've resigned myself to it, but not Georges, for he ruptures himself trying to drag a smile out of her.

"What's the use?" I harp. "When she doesn't want, it's a waste."

But Georges he reckons it'll come, it's just a matter of trust, and he asks me to set about entertaining her, but there's no use ferreting in my brain, there's never a thing I can do for Vulva.

It's true that mornings when she comes in unexpected when we're eating breakfast and the youngsters is still asleep and it's still almost dark, she has no choice but to say what brought her, so she asks for a drink of milk or an aspirin, and it's Georges gets up, for I'm wise to her already and I waste no energy on her whims.

At the very start of her coming home, yes, just looking at her there in the sheets, lying with the face different and the hair longer and the blubber all gone, I could persuade myself she'd changed, I could believe it was another person they'd sent us, and perhaps it's possible I said to myself inward: "Maybe she's changed, Vulva," and "Maybe she'll behave decent, and work hard," or "Maybe we'll have a bit of peace and quiet?"

But after I got used I could see clear that maybe she's a different Vulva outside, though inside she's the same as ever, still my Vulva, just worse than the old one maybe due to the belly.

That belly, no one's ever been able to see it, not never, neither the track of the scars nor the big ball that's vanished into nothing, but that's the only thing you hear about, so you'd fancy the whole world of the farm turns on it: you have to never hurry poor little Vulva on account of the belly, you have to never upset her, she has to never carry anything, she has to never get hurt, and all the things obsess the minds of even the youngsters so they gawp at her front when she goes past.

What is there so special about that belly of hers anyway? Aside from it taking in my seeds to breed half-wits, it's a regular belly, there's nothing to differ it from the belly of any other hussy that's had a ball of her own there and the surgeon's knife and the hospital chemistry.

This whole ball business, I've always mistrusted that it's just an excuse dreamed up for getting away. Maybe it was just a leave Vulva took, maybe she just went off like on a trip or for a holiday, for when she was showing off the ball, when she pointed to how it was getting bigger, it was always under the top and you could never feel it bare naked in her meat.

That seems queer to me, when I think about it.

So where can she have spent the days she was away, Vulva, with maybe some other male diddling her from behind and letting her have her fifteen minutes of sport? So now she has no wish to come home and find her spouse toiling at the hay with the sweat of his forehead, dark rings under his armpits, and a true honest face clean of suspicion, and his arms reached out in welcome, and that's why she looks so sour, for she remembers about that time she had her freedom away off the farm.

At that juncture in my reflection Georges comes in shouting am I there Paul? and I shout back: "Inside at the hay," and he takes over my spot to bring me up on the party and its arrangements.

There'll be orangeade, for Georges he knows how to make it and it'll leave the youngsters no excuse to swill any wine, but he'll have to buy what he needs for it, but it won't cost dear.

On top of that we have to decide about settling the menu for the main course, for Georges he reckons two or three chips isn't enough to satisfy a man nor a woman neither, and there Georges gives a laugh—he gives a false laugh every time he says "woman," for that floozy of his is shunning him: since Vulva's home again Georges has no time for her any more, but Georges he thinks it's nothing but a jealous fit she'll get over by Christmas, and he lets on he's laughing off, but the chin it twitches and shows a trembling from major upset and weariness.

But that's not what I'm curious for: it's to know if ever he saw the stitching on the belly?

"No," he answers, surprised at what I'm raising, and he keeps on about the party, so I say I've no wish to have guests no more, for with just us on the farm already there's plenty for a party.

Georges he doesn't agree: the more there is the merrier, and all them ones is polite, they never pay Vulva no attention at all, they just come to fill their glasses and they hardly ever even take a squy at her.

Georges he figures no doubt he can tell what's acceptable or hateful to hear, he fancies he knows what he has to say to maneuver like he wants, but it's a different problem torturing me deep inside: it means near nothing now if Charles goes sweet-talking her or some other fat-ass tickles her fancy if Vulva never had a thing in the belly but a potato stuck up the dress or a beet or who knows maybe an old apple.

Even just thinking about that belly brings a flood of pictures of the first nights of the wedding, of the first night from before she was mine and I put the ring on her: now there's no pickers left in the farmyard except one hurrying late to catch the mail bus, with the old man squying after her and remarking to his Paul that to look at her you'd say there was a frog would have a juicy piece of leg on her . . . And Paul leaping into the yard and turning his charm on the lady, and she not wanting to talk, and there comes the bus, and Paul leaning on the gate to bar, and her that's not Vulva yet but she's sobbing like she knows already, and Paul taking her by the waist and leading her into the kitchen, and the old codger laughing away to himself, and the three glasses of plum, with her never touching, Pa, the eyes like she never notices, Paul making nice, the bed, the bedroom, and the old bugger coughing in the wall, and her not wanting, and the star of her hair, the "no," the belly, and Vulva's rosy pink, and then afterwards us chatting a bit more, and then looking in the morning, and it's her . . .

Seeing me off in the moon like that, Georges he gets a fright it's no normal absence and I've turned funny in the head, so he prods to wake me and he asks if everything's okay, is everything okay, Paul?

I answer: "Well yes, it's fine," but it just stirs up memories down deep of stooping over the belly, and it slows me down so the words fall heavy in the empty space.

But Georges then, no doubt made bold, for likely it's his encouragement to make a move, to reveal intimacies, he makes free to ask about my mother, if she sometimes rises up in my memory, seeing that for a long time now Georges hasn't dared ask that question and all the talk has been about Pa, so it's been a problem for Georges to know who was wife to my father and what became of the good lady I owe the light of day to, but doubtless she's up with the angels by this time.

"Well, that's a tough one to answer," I say to Georges, but it's no use resisting: it brings back memories, ones you've shut out, ones you turned away from except to shout out in the dark of night, but it's a nightmare then, so I just stand gawp-mouthed and I say: "Well . . . well . . ." thinking of the lap and all the clouts.

Meantime Georges explains about his wee mama, for his pa's dead and gone, but his mama's still with him, old now, and she reared the lot of them by herself, him, his sister, and his brother, but Georges has to cut short, for a voice comes asking: "Can I come in?" and he walks into the barn, and it's one of the them that comes representing.

We're already insured all we need, I say, for fire, death, and water, but he says that's not what he's come about, and he opens his suitcase on the ground, and it's full of knives, all polished and shiny, from the smallest to the biggest. Georges he goes "Wow!" and the rep says it's due to the factory going broke and he has to dispose of them before he leaves the country, so he has a case-full reduced to half price.

"Fifty percent off, then?" says Georges, and the rep goes yes, and he can offer a special reduction just for us.

"Well, the trouble is we're not used . . . " I start off, and he says that doesn't matter and of course, them being of such a high quality, his knives, we can cut through anything we like, something hard, something real tough, right to the bone, animal's throats even if you like, for that's a job it's best to do yourself, but I say we've no need for we have Jules on the spot: Jules, he's like the butcher for around here, like a real one except he slaughters on the side just to oblige folk and out of personal interest, but when he's killing the animals he hurts them, and in the house even you can hear them bawling.

Georges, it's more than he can stand to miss out on new goods at the factory price, so he turns over the handles between his fingers and asks how much apiece.

"But we've no call for any," I tug at him behind, so then Georges stands up, but the rep says it's no matter, for his car trunk's full of other surprises, like computers, now there's a useful item on a farm for sure.

We go to take a look-see in the car, it's filled with all kinds of gizmos, kitchen appliances that can only bring joy to the lady of the house, and Georges says there's great deals, it's all quality stuff, but it's too dear for yours truly.

The rep collects up his suitcase: he passes by this way often and he'll stop in next time too, always with great offers and brand new goods, well worth the money, and it costs nothing to look, so we go courteous: "Drop in any time." We slam his car door shut and watch him turn, but then at the last before he's gone Georges he settles on a penknife.

30

She's sitting with her hands under the table, Vulva, wondering what we're hatching, for now she talks sometimes, just short.

All the lanterns is hung in the branches except the ones the youngsters burned up chasing over the fields, so when the big day comes and we want lights in the leaves there's only three or four blackened ones left with already the candles burned down to stumps.

"It's a bad start," I remark to Georges, but he reckons with the three lanterns it's enough for us to see our drinking glasses and there's no need to give the youngsters a licking right off like I'm setting to, seeing the others will be coming soon and there's nothing on the table yet.

Me, Georges, Claudie, and Vulva, that makes four of us, plus Charles if the humor takes him, and the youngsters will swarm down like locusts to pick at their portions, so I get five glasses from the sideboard and Georges the plates and chairs.

It's salt cod we're feeding on.

For ten people Georges had said at first, but I said that was too many for the room available, so he dropped to seven or eight and we settled on five, seeing our Vulva has to be happy at the people coming, and Jean-Robert and Richard aren't close with her. We have to feel easy, and Vulva won't if there's strangers fussing about asking her what she's drinking, or worse, and some coming just to find out where the animals is and where's the lady of the house and how it happened she was cured and what happened to her lumpiness, and other unpleasantness that makes so you can't feel at home having a drink content in peace and quiet by yourself.

The codfish, it's soaking in the bucket to lose its salt into the solution. Georges he took a long trip to find one nice enough to be worth gorging ourselves on, but when he got back it was cut into slabs already so me and the youngsters we was all disappointed that Georges didn't come carrying a whole critter home but just white squares in his paws.

We're tripping over the youngsters, and even Georges that usual can keep gentle and hold his patience and stay nice, he cuffs them on the backside to stop them coming like mice to peek in the sauce and skew the lids.

One of them has been set on watch in the cow barn to raise the alarm if Jasmine takes a notion to calve in the straw, for according to the vet that comes to feel her over each week it's near to coming, and even it could maybe be tonight, though it'd be a terrible pity if it caused us to miss a grand party the likes of which, he says, hasn't been seen on this farm for years, and him dawdling on with his flatteries hoping to get invited, but when you know from hearsay the way he can knock off the bottle it's better to bid him goodbye, hand him over his banknote, and never let on you know right well why he carries on about the lovely smell, and you shove him into his jeep, goodbye and thank you mister vet, safe drive.

Little by little the party gets off the ground: me spinning like a top in the yard gathering up the cocks and hens to shut them up in their boards, me spinning like a top at the table and roaring after the youngsters to help, Georges in a twist in the kitchen, the codfish in its brine, the wine bottles chilling, fine clear weather overhead for the evening with the first of the stars and the moon slender like a finger-clipping, and Vulva all droopy asking out in her flat voice what we're up to, but no one bothering to answer.

Final, there's one thing troubles me all the same, and I say: "Georges," once the table looks nice with everything in the right place, the salt and pepper out, the bread, the tablecloth, and all lit up under the trees even though the daylight's still alive, then, "who's going to break it to Vulva?"

Georges he's of a mind it's him should announce the party to her, seeing all the same it's in the kitchen the best touches is put, but me I've a more joyous notion fermenting for us to tell her all together.

"You see," I paint for him, "we'll all go together to Vulva, along with the youngsters." Of course Vulva she'll ask what's stewing and we'll all shout together: "Welcome home Vulva!" and the wee ones will give her a hug, for she has her uses as a mother to them all the same. "What do you think?" I go to Georges, and Georges he gets all enthusiastic at the idea, so you'd fancy these days is building an influence over him.

Georges just suggests we wait till Claudie turns up with Charles so we can start off the party all bonded together like one.

"Okay," I grant, "but that floozy of yours had better get a move on," pointing to my wrist, "for she's a good half hour late," seeing it's half seven already.

It's no matter, says Georges, for in his country being late is nothing unusual, and anyway on the kitchen stove there's nothing ready yet, but it doesn't matter, and he suggests we get things going by pouring ourselves a glass right off, just to get off the ground, so we pull the cork and drink, and at that moment of enjoyment there's a yell erupts on us from the yard, it's the young one left on watch raising the alarm for Jasmine, for there's a shifting in her belly and it's serious for sure, for the cow's roaring from pain in the straw.

"It's just the labor starting up, it's not like a fire we have to rush off to," I say calm, me with my glass to my lips and Georges pouring another brimmer, but this young one he kicks up a real fuss and drags at my shirt never minding the clout I land, till I've to tell Georges: "I won't be long, just keep an eye on the bottles," for already there's a couple of crashers come, a few sly buggers that smelled the drink from far, but it's alarm over nothing.

As soon as they catch on what's up the wee ones is after me on my heels, though I tell them to scat and threaten a licking, for Jasmine having it hard to calve is no sight for young eyes, and it'd be more of a help if they went to see if maybe Georges can make use of them, but in the cow barn when we go in there's already a few on the spot and it's past time for scolding, seeing Jasmine is ready to have her calf, and already it's even urgent to help her, for the poor thing is suffering, you can see just from the death in her eye.

"Oho there my beauty," it comes over me murmuring, "it's a rough go this," and tender I wipe the sweat off her and I take hold of the bottle I'd hid in my shirt and I draw the stopper, "Here, drink this my dancer," I say, sticking the neck between her teeth, and I push her to drink, though it burns and brings out like tears, for to her it tastes just the same as to folks: before they know all the good it does they balk, and it's only after the scorch they feel the benefit, and then they get a major thirst for more.

Then I go to look what's showing at the rump. The passage is big enough, almost big enough to let a little one out.

I rub her on the paunch with the alcohol till it gives me a thirst too, and I remember the party we're having that evening, and I ask the young ones what's going on, and the young ones, for they know everything like they've got aerials and pick up the news everywhere they go, they say they're stuffing themselves back there with Vulva at the table and Georges guzzling away, well past his first slice, and some is making fun of the fish.

"And Claudie?" I'm surprised.

None answers, they just keep mum, so I go again: "And Claudie?"

Well, Claudie, says one of them, she hasn't turned up for the party, and all the others go yes yes, it's Vulva's fault, due to Georges neglecting Claudie and spending no time with her any more, but it's a good thing the men is there, for the young ones they find that fish meat real gross.

"The men?" I go controlled, but the blood's already pumped up in me. "So they're not on their own, Georges and Vulva?"

Well no, there's the men you sometimes see around the farm, and the youngsters say when they came to say hi at the gate Vulva told them to sit down and eat, and Georges said there was plenty for all and they should sit down, they'd make room, and there's been a good bit of the red swilled down already.

They're probably some gawpers Georges has drummed up for the party due to the shortage of guests after the no-show by Charles and his woman, so my mind's set easy, and then I say: "Quiet!" for the labor's starting up again and the cow's getting worked up.

Then there comes a violent convulsion and the cow goes into a fit, and it relaxes off, but soon it grips her again, but my girls they're so brave they let the calf rupture them yet they never let out a sigh nor the least of a roar. It's only from seeing the way it ripples under their coats you can tell the hammering they take.

The youngsters is in awe too and feel the stress and they move away in the straw, for they're scared stiff Jasmine will die on us.

But me I'm used, I know for sure it'll come out all right in the end and it has to torment her, due to the Bible where it's written: "In pain thou shalt bring forth children," as I explain to the wee ones all this time in the cow barn, along with a lot of other beneficial things, and if Georges only heard he'd be pleased at the talk.

Anyway it's a surprise Georges hasn't shown his mug yet, for he's of a nature curious to go poking into every corner, but it's no time to be dwelling on that, for it'll soon be ready to come out.

The youngsters is holding the ropes I keep hanging precious on their nails in case of a hitch, when you need the vet but he's not available, and I can see for myself there's help needed, for the calf's showing its feet but no legs and my beauty's wore out, so I roll up my sleeve and I stick my arm in like I've seen the vet doing and like I've often had to undertake myself, so I pull the head and turn the way I can feel it has to sit to come out, and I get it out nice and easy with the youngsters squawking at all the blood.

I lower the baby down on the straw.

Jasmine's still spitting wads so we take off the halter, and then she moos content like a woman and a mother fulfilled, and I stroke her belly, her back, her nose and her neck, and it's like I'm saying: "I'm pleased with you, old girl."

There's the calf all shivery, for he's chilly outside of his mother. I lift him up to Jasmine and she smells him and licks him, for she has to be real happy at calving a wee one like that.

"What's the matter, Pa?" says one of the youngsters squying at me, and I bawl: "Quiet now!" for my calf wants peace and quiet, and if they have to act their circus they should do it outside, for there's privacy needed here for the two to get acquainted, and if there's too much ruckus it covers the signs and maybe Jasmine she'll forget she's just given birth, with it still shivering wet on the straw.

Then the youngsters go quiet, but some want to know if it's a he, while the calf's getting on its feet, and what's it called.

The baby he latches on the teats for he knows right off how to go about sucking the cow's milk, and now she has her head low over the straw, like it was all just a day's work.

Someone pushes open the door.

"Everything okay here?" and there comes a laugh, and it's Georges gives a slap on your shoulder and exclaims it's a real beauty, a red one like that, and he tickles its star with never a thought he's meddling with it suckling the teats.

Vulva, she shows her snout in the rear holding a plate in one hand: Georges he thought they'd bring out my portion for me, there being no sign of me back at the house. It's still near luke-warm and I'm glad of it, but at the first fork in the mouth the stomach rebels against letting in the cod: it's due to the cows, the calf, and the over-emotion from what happened in the cow barn and what's left on the ground.

"He's a real handsome fellow, this little Codfish," Georges he laughs, squatted down and never caring the straw's a browny-red, "He's a real good-looking little guy," tugging him by the ear, and what's not normal, the little runt still not an hour in the cow barn he turns to Georges and sucks on his finger.

31

Each morning comes up it's me puts them out to grass. Me, when there's a newborn, I never leave to anyone else to look after the mother and child. There's some that confuse and mix the animals up, never caring that they get jealous and bear grudges like little girls that rob the dolls off one another to play mothers.

Jasmine's making good headway, all lovely and docile, and well recovered from the calving, with Codfish running after her all staggery like he's drunk. He's had only five days on this earth.

They've got their own special patch near the farmhouse, full of good grass, tender green like hoarfrost and rich for the mother to recruit up her strength and her vitamins, and for her to run healthy milk at the teats for her baby that doesn't touch the grassy tufts yet, and for the sun to soften her coat.

The vet he comes now and again to make sure all's going right and collect his banknote. I had to tell over again the story of the calving with all the details on how long it lasted, and the expulsion, and show how with my hand I turned inside to help the little tyke come out.

If you're a vet it gives you no joy to hear someone else can do your job a lot better than you and manage without your help and get away without paying, but this one he keeps pally and coming back to the farm, for every time he's leaving Georges pokes him in the ribs and asks: "A little bit of fish for the doctor?" or maybe: "A little plateful for the road?" seeing he has enough over from the party to last weeks, for the youngsters won't touch it, nor will Vulva, for she says it gives her acid, and me barely neither, for I'm not so keen on the smell, and the vet he says: "All right, but just a little piece," and then he sits at the table a whole hour long, for he's thick as thieves with Georges, like everyone Georges casts his spell on.

What he likes to tell is the surprise he got the day after the party when he came to the farm to see after Jasmine and he found the yard total deserted and the hens still shut in and the young ones at their jinks, and Georges he laughs remembering how we rose late due to the drink at the party and all the guests and the way the cows brought him out at near eleven roaring their complaints.

"It's then your wife comes out, I'm sorry but I've forgot her name," the vet says, "opening the door and asking what I want," and he said he'd come about Jasmine, but the lady said it was too late, it was all over and done with proper and by the rules.

Then he toasts to the lady, he drinks to the calf and the mother, and says he has jobs to do, but that's a lie, for he dawdles on a long while more.

When he saw Codfish he found he'd a good coat on him and he was well put together, steady on his legs and good-looking, all things I knew already with no need for any calculations to see he's a charmer with all you can ask for in an animal.

That calf, it's a love-affair between him and me, who knows why. I've put a pile of them through my hands since I've been bringing them into the world, since I've been making them all come out down through that same tunnel, but none's ever had the same effect on the master as this Codfish: when we see each other we greet, his coat gets a rub, he gives a good lick and maybe a moo with a switch of the tail, and a little salt gets doled out, though it's not advised and normal forbidden, and though Jasmine looks hurt if she's left out.

It's why at the outset I wasn't keen for Georges to baptize him after that word. Me, I said: "Let's call him Crossbow instead," and always when I was talking I'd say: "Crossbow's grown already," or: "I'm off to see about Crossbow," to get everyone's hearing used to it, but it was too late already after Georges he said in the straw: "He's a good-looker, this Codfish," and kept on repeating the label, and Georges is a bigger talker and the young ones listen to him for he never gives them a licking, so they all took after him, and from hearing "Codfish" here and "Codfish" there the boss himself broke down and gave in, for if it's called twenty different names you can't be sure any more which one you're talking about and it's a detriment for the farm. But when you're alone with him in private in the cow barn there's nothing to stop you calling him pet names, like "Little one," or "Princess," or "Tiger," going on like some old bugger that's lost his head over a beast.

Codfish being a young calf with no experience and naïve like he is, he's easy to fool, and he responds to Vulva and falls for her when she comes to him almost every day putting her airs across him. For you have to grant Vulva's wild about him too, and there's a tight scrap every day to see who'll put him in the shed or give him the bottle when Jasmine has trouble providing.

He has to get used to dealing with other people and learn how the world is and all the false things in it, I tell myself hard-hearted, and it forges your character to see others than your ma and pa, yet it tears the face off me to see the way Vulva comes revolving around him and the calf making so much of her, like there was ever a thing but harm to be gotten from her.

Vulva on her side tries every trick to win him over, always out in the field whispering flatteries and scratching him, though he'd far rather you let him skip about to build his muscles. For sure she spoils him as soon as my back's turned and stuffs him with treats to get him in her pocket. Whenever I can I stop and give her my mind, but it's not often I've the chance to go by, for when you're out in the fields there's not often a break to leave Georges and go to see if Vulva's behaving straight and true.

It's like the night of the party. When we got back dog-weary from the birth, what did we find but Vulva's admirers still all sitting at the table in raptures over her ladyship, but acting all modest to reassure and maybe almost apologetic, so you almost didn't dare shake hands with sorts you barely knew to see, and you stood there looking at the wine-bottles all emptied shameless, and Vulva cooing there with their eyes in a ring about her, flies sitting on her meat, till final Georges says: "But come and sit yourself down too, Paul," clearing me room on the bench for my ass.

"We'd no notion of such a treasure!" one of them he says with a laugh.

"A lady like that, and kept secret!" says the other with some help from the red no doubt, and them all laughing their heads off and others too going on about it being worth the trip just to see the lady, and complimenting too that she's not just worth looking at, but on top of that she has a lot upstairs, what's not expected from the fair sex, and all of them laughing over theirs that's keeping house back home.

At the start I asked myself: what they're doing here under my lanterns, all these males stuck on my Vulva like flies, but I caught on after a bit when she started opening her trap and bringing out her dribs of words with them all quivering eager for what's coming out of her gob. For sure what has them all a-tremble and abuzz is Vulva starting to tattle, a secret Vulva from years back that suddenly starts blabbing and pulling back the veil in spite of her husband's protests, and clucking like a pullet, and what do you see going by but scraps of Vulva, memories of the times before she came to us, and from before the ball in her innards and the microbes she hatched on us, like she was able to remember and it was fascinating.

Seeing all the same I'm not listening and there's nothing I don't know already about the things she's embroidering up, and anyway me being in all modesty the initiator of the whole story and not able to stand that slobbery voice of hers, all the time she was talking I could easy watch the way the eyes was busy ferreting bold as brass in her bosom, but even so it's not as full and you can't see the curves as good.

Thing is, she'd still be good stuff, Paul's Vulva, thing is them neighbor sorts is drooling in their beards to have her so handy here, thing is they're telling themselves damn but he's a lucky dog that can grab a handful of her in bed whenever the fancy takes him. For curves and thighs is things men spot quick, the kind that gets spread far around, and they know from signs, just like a fox for hens, and even ones maybe not from around here, ones from some other part of the country, they can feel right off, just looking, when they pass in sight of a roof, that there's a good-looking lady in the place. For my Vulva there, there's no remedy, they're all green from wanting her, you just need to see that nice balcony up front and that rear end spread under the table, even after the disease, even after the surgeon and the hospital, it's still the same grand lump that sleeps at Paul's, for he has taste in the fair sex, not like them losers.

Then the urge came over me, but strangled quick, choked off and shrunk away, to grab our Vulva by the arm and say to her: "Come on, forget them dead losses," and haul her off into the dark in the face of all decency and hospitality.

But just then the dark one stood up to drink a toast and went: "To the lady's good health!"

"To her good health!" they all went, and then another stood up: "To the mistress of the farm!"

And then another one laughing: "To her lovely name!"

And others: "To the ladies!"

"To lovely ladies!"

And another again: "To the former patient!"

"To her new belly!" they all shouted together, for Vulva had told about her experience, and all of them they kept on giving their best wishes till they sang a song and then another, and then finally one of the ones you're not supposed to sing in female company, and you'd have said the party was in full swing.

With all the glasses raised and toasts drunk it didn't take long to get the worse for weather and there was a few had to get up quick and stoop over in the dark, but no matter, Georges said when he saw me upset, for as long as it goes on the ground it's first-class fertilizer.

Then Georges introduced to me a young fellow fancying I'd be interested, a lad, Georges he said, that has bright ideas on how to work with technology, and this one began to tell how such and such a machine works and explain the importance for the quality of the first growth, and all the time I'm listening, or letting on I am, at the other end of the table Vulva started chatting with two males that look like they've a heap of intentions.

If you ask me, she's enjoying herself fine, I thought to myself, me giving continual a loud "yeah" back to the lad, or sometimes a chance "no, no," or "uhuh?" or "is that so?" and "really?" and so on, and he never noticed I couldn't care less for his blather.

What in God's name could they be telling her that has her splitting herself laughing? I pricked an ear. Where could she have gotten to know them? Didn't they have their two hands under the table? And all such kinds of theories that set you stewing, so I didn't know no more what to think, and just then Georges he came asking "Is there any bottles left?" so I got up to take a look, and when I came back up from the cellar there was nor hair nor hide of Vulva to be seen at her end of the table, nothing but a couple of empties and a full, and no sign of the males neither, but something told me for the reassurance: "Likely she's in the orchard answering the call of nature, or maybe she drank too much and she's throwing up."

"Yes, but where's the two males?" it occurred to me, and just then the young lad was saying it made no difference to the plants if they was hoed one by one or by the acre, so you had to turn back and let on you understood.

It's real nice of us, the young lad said, to have put on a little party like this one, and it was the vet let the cat out, for they heard by rumor and they all came right off, like they always do when there's a shindig going, and what a great sort he is, that vet.

Was that maybe the sound of someone calling out? But no one budges, they're all hammered on the red, and maybe I'm hearing things, but the worry's still churning and prodding to picture the way our Vulva is lying out there with one or two or three males on top of her, asking for more and shouting out: "Come on!" and "Giddy up!"

Isn't that someone bawling out? What's more, this dark is a godsend when you're tumbling in the grass a few yards off from your lawful spouse, but the young one he starts up again his sermon about the machines, so what's left to make the night fade away but drink and fill up again?

Then I had to get up and go to the gate to say goodnight to them jokers that's so glad they've gotten to know my good lady they'd heard so much about, and then I saw her busy saying goodbye to three or four hanging round her apron strings, and one making free to give her a peck and saying: "Goodbye," likely fancying she's for him.

Georges he said: "I'm sleepy," and went in a zigzag off to his glasshouse. Vulva she headed for her bed, likely real wore out. I landed a few clouts on the young ones escaped from their bedclothes, tidied away five or six glasses and some litter, closed the doors and windows, and then with no further recourse I went to stretch out.

32

The day he came, I remember like yesterday, we said with Georges: "Till the end of summer, and after that we'll handle the whole thing ourselves, for a farmhand costs."

There he is inside the glasshouse packing his bag.

"Don't forget to take the overalls and the shirts," I go to remind of what he hung out to dry, and Georges he nods yes, a silent yes, and for two or three days he has hardly been able to get a word out, like from a heavy dose of weariness.

"Need some help?" I ask, just to be polite one last time, and then I go: "Georges old pal, you'll be missed when the glasshouse is empty," real happy to raise his spirits, but Georges he lets out a sigh and carries on silent, so I say loud for the youngsters that have their noses flat to the glass: "Isn't that right children, this here farmhand he'll be missed after he's off on the bus?" but not one of them gives a grunt.

We had to find out the timetable of arrivals and departures from the farm, first for the bus and then for the train and the planes that take off direct for the South, and Georges said he'd found a fast timetable, and then he let out a sigh and said his words over again about how it was a shame, how now wasn't the right time for him to be leaving, and all them lamentations that's useless except for sowing discomfort in souls, seeing the decision's made and now it's a duty.

All summer I'd warned: "End of summer, Georges, end of summer," and he'd always nodded agreed with his big toasted cheeks, so you'd have thought he understood all right and had no doubts left, but then the other evening he says, Georges, in the slack of our talk, when we was still round the table with the young ones outside shouting in the dark at pulling the legs off grasshoppers: "Summer will soon be done," so it leaves me no choice but to say: "It's time for you to be going, then . . ." and be forced to stick to it, never mind that Georges turns pale, never mind he says the time's not right, never mind he clenches his hand tight on the glass and makes free to say maybe it's too early to be announcing to him sudden like that, so I have to repeat, I have to spell out, though it's hard on me: "It's almost come, the time for you to go . . ." though with Vulva unfit it's no way convenient me being left to do all the work myself.

With Georges we've had good times on this farm, I'm not one to deny it. A farmhand was a real help, especial this year with Vulva playing the fine lady on us: he worked all on his own with no feet-dragging or being loath that it's not work for a man, and better even than her, if I can speak my mind frank. But once the deadline's set you can hardly shift again, for it doesn't look professional, and maybe after you've changed the date the farmhand he'll take into his head he just needs to please you for you to keep him the whole year round, and then he'll go slacking off in the spot you heat free of charge for him like it's his own place, and in winter it costs to feed a huge lump like that. "Anyway, in the glasshouse it's chilly in autumn," was the argument I put in as well for him not to think it depends just on me, and for him to remember there's seasons, that the climate changes, and before you know the weather will turn frosty.

"Okay," says Georges in front of his suitcase that's spilling over, and he takes a squy round the glasshouse and just says "I think I've forgotten nothing," and I check too out of the corner of my eye that he's robbing nothing on loan from us.

On the nail there's the shirt, the one with the hole that was lent him one day it was raining and Georges came in soaked after working hard, and it'd be a fine gesture to let him have it as a souvenir for thinking of the farm, but it still can always come in handy if we run out and Vulva's late with the wash, and besides there's already the sum you have to fork over for the summer.

"Here's the total," I say, laying out the banknotes end to end on the mattress for him to see all his sweated toil lined up, and the cost of a farmhand.

"Minus the board," I itemize for him, "and minus the lodging," in case he'd fancy there was a mistake, "and minus for the plum," to let him know as well I've counted all the empties he's left behind, "and less for Vulva's flowers," to show who's got good memory and recollects the whole business. Jorge he takes the five notes: "Thanks," he says with a tight mouth, and he's worried about the time, so I hunt the young ones to go and look on the kitchen clock in case he'd chance missing the bus and be left on our hands, for now his gear's all cleared out we'll take the mattress away to make room for the winter.

As we're crossing the yard a window budges and Vulva shows her nose.

"The farmhand's off," I say joyful, like I'm announcing good news, in case Vulva she being so sensitive she'd start spewing her tears that can stream rivers before you know it, and Vulva she looks down at him, and the farmhand he lifts his hand too and signs to Vulva he's off, and he blows her a kiss, and maybe it's nothing but a goodbye.

We walk on to the gate, and I reckon it's none of my concern any farther, seeing from here on outside it's no longer my property.

"Goodbye, Jorge," I say using his own name for a little considerate kindness, and truth to tell he's been useful on the farm. "Give them all our best," though I've no notion who I'm talking about, and I shake hands and watch him go off with the suitcase on one side and all the youngsters trotting after, like the king and his courtiers.

The farmhand he sets down the suitcase at the sign, and you can hear the roar of the bus coming, appearing, getting bigger, and pulling up at the stop, Jorge getting in, paying the fare with the coins he'd gotten ready, and the bus starting off in its din.

Summer came, and then the hay-making, and here you are with September almost done, and the farmhand's hardly here before he's off.

The youngsters come back to the farmhouse. A good slap round the ears helps them walk faster and make up their minds to lend a hand in the cow barn. And now Vulva she owes us a hand at the work too. So I go to fetch her from the bedroom.

The door's locked. Knock knock I go on the doorframe, but there's nothing stirs.

I go out of pure politeness: "Is there anyone inside?" and at the same time I push down the handle, but it won't open.

"Open up now, Vulva," I get impatient, "or there'll be trouble."

The hussy is moving about inside.

"I know you're in there," I say like in the movies. "What kind of a carry-on is this, shutting yourself in?" and "Come on Vulvia," for all the time mistaken I'm talking to her like I'm from the South, and just when I'm not expecting and I've turned to leave, Vulva she says through that she's not going to open.

"Why not?" I ask.

Vulva, she never answers.

"Don't I treat you nice then?"

No answer.

"Don't I treat you nice, all you ask for?"

Vulva she starts up the usual whingeing that she gets no respect, she's not treated like a lady, the same jeremiahs she's dished up ever since the hospital and isn't worth bending an ear to, so I justify back to her that already bedsheets and blankets is too good for a hussy like her that queens it the way she does, never counting, I say to myself, that she never performs her due to her husband, her wifely due. It's what I figure, but I tell her out loud she's extravagating, and then I add that I'll wait till she shuts her trap, for I'm deaf, and at that she goes mum, at least till the next time.

If she wants us to go at it, I laugh to myself inward, she only needs to open up wide, she just has to let the dog see the rabbit to remember what it's like when you're caring proper for your lady: me, this whole business of respect for women gets me roiled down below, rousing me like the notion of setting at it, seeing after all she's mine and that's what she's here for, make no mistake.

I put on my honey-sweet voice and I slip in: "Wouldn't you'd like a wee nap?"

That's the way I express whenever I get the urge, though it's rare, and Vulva knows I always convey the suggestion discreet, since the day she first came to my bed not out of weariness and hardly defended herself, for when I make an effort to make tender like that, in spite of the detriment to me with the work that's left hanging, maybe there's something carries across, like caresses, and maybe it makes a woman feel good. But she acts all innocent, the stubborn carp, like she can't remember what a "wee nap" means and thinks it's just shutting your eyes and dreaming, and she laughs back that it's broad daylight. I query again if maybe she's feeling the lack of a husband owing to his masculine function, and she goes with a laugh that no, that she feels no lack nor need of anything except a little space and peace and quiet, and then I bawl out for her to stick her esteem she knows where and her respect between her tits, and tearing mad I say too the thing Pa said on his deathbed, to watch out for that poison meat for she's a rot in the home, and then I clear off.

It's easy for Georges to advise being nice to your wife and keep her company when he himself has no real one at home to answer no and laugh at him on account every time you try to get snug it's never right.

When I get to my cow barn there's not a single one of them at work, they're all fussing over the animals stroking them from horn to tail, teasing them with handfuls of hay when they need none and just want to be left in peace and quiet.

"Scat the lot of you," I go angry, threatening with the pitchfork, and they scamper, all but one of the big ones that shows a finger and says "asshole" before he scrams for fear I'd land him one.

It's not true what Vulva says, that she feels no lack, that she's not pining from longing for a man, for she feels it a whole pile, that's as sure as can be since the time she went off to be a patient and after came back home more thin and pale. That was just a woman's scheme that was weary of her man and wanted a taste of less stale, that was feeling for a change, a change of husbands for example, or maybe just to treat herself to a few younger bucks.

You just had to see, the evening before, when the farmhand gave the firm confirmation he was taking the plane, the way Vulva said right out, just like it came to her natural, though normal it's like pulling teeth: "We'll never see you again, Georges . . ." and how Georges answered it was a shame, and you could feel the awkwardness at me being there watching and listening, so Georges he said: "Isn't that a noise in the barn?" and then after a minute: "Did I tell you Blossom was spitting blood?"

But I smelt his dodge all right and I said it was just the wind whistling in the boards and Blossom was likely having the monthlies out the front, and I stayed glued there between the two of them never missing a trick and listening for what they'd say, the my God poor Georges would be missed for sure, and the lady shouldn't worry, they'd write epistles to one another, and then going quiet and later the same words phrased different that gave the impression of a longing to say more but the boss was there.

But in the end I had to go out, seeing that the young ones is just a pester since they've been set to work, making a shambles all over the farmyard, for they're not fit even to throw slop to the cats. Every evening they go calling me out with the excuse there's something broken or gone off track, the big gate not closing right, the key going lost and no spare, or some animal misbehaving, or one gone missing, or a milk can turned over by magic, or pitchforks they can never find in the straw. I do my job putting everything back in shape, clearing the mess and pulling their hair to teach them the way to work, so that the day Paul's put in his coffin the whole undertaking don't go to pot and the animals don't quit their good healthy life-habits.

So in the time it takes me going and coming, rounding up the young ones and laying out my threats, two good quarter hours have gone, and as soon as I get inside again there's an atmosphere hits me, with Georges all natural at the table and Vulva all natural across on the other side like they never shifted, except Georges is a lovely red in the mug and there's a button open on the dress, and never an eye straight at you but just deceiving looks.

"Is everything going like you want?" I asked sarcastic, and for vengeance that the farmhand was losing the game for Vulva due to having to go. Georges he acted surprised and said they was waiting on me for the cheese, as if he'd ever given a rat's fart for the master's comings and goings when food's concerned.

Then we had that evening. For the first time since he came, the farmhand, and I reckon even since Vulva drew her first breath on the farm, she agreed to let plum in her glass, and Paul even took advantage to pour her a brimmer, and it was from that the first big scrap grew, for Vulva she didn't want to finish it and she threatened to get up, and Georges to settle it he took a fair share from her, but I went cursing against females, how it's wasted when all they want is to dip their tongues in it, and everything she does is a sham, Vulva, and then she started bawling, and Georges said we should cool down considering it was like an impromptu party to mark the occasion of his departure.

"But I'm cooled down, so I am," I say to Georges with a laugh, taking a drag on one I'd lit for myself, and Vulva she goes out saying something we can't even catch for her bawling, and Georges he chases to bring her back, and they fuss in the passage for an age if you ask me, and Vulva then back at the table with her cackle cut and not wanting to look Paul in the eye. And her furious that Paul wants her to force herself to taste it, and teasing her a bit, saying: "Come on now," to get her to down just one mouthful, and gripping to force her mouth open, and Vulva spewing it back at him, and then there was the slaps, the boot, the licking, a real set-to, a pasting plus a clout or two, till Georges drags me off her, and he was right, for the way it stings the eyes it can turn you crazy as a wild beast.

So maybe it was the right time for Georges to go and leave the two of us to settle the whole thing and work out face to face and knock things back into shape. It's maybe why at the door, I see clear now, the notion came over me to pay her attentions and lie with her, not out of any real wanting, though that comes with custom, but to get things patched up between the parties and stitch them together between the sheets, just like the late lamented Georges advised.

33

In the trees there's still two lanterns left spreading their light and lending a kind of summer soul, for in spite of the chill evenings, and though it's good to keep yourself dressed warm in wool, me it's still out front I'd rather smoke as long as winter hasn't come with its vexations. As long as I stay out there it reminds me of the grand days with the farmhand and the joyous atmosphere there was, instead of the dreariness now and me reflecting with no one to hear. It's the nostalgic time of year when you have all the same chores and work to get through but the body feels degrees lower, and the soul too, seeing they're connected, and it's due to the sun hardly showing itself, for it's away over other countries where it's spring. Them's the kind of things I reflect to myself, and that you're entitled to be idle on the eve of the day the Lord forbids working from dawn.

The young ones is amusing themselves after the insects, you sometimes see Vulva going by in her old apron, though it's supper time, inspecting the chrysanthemum beds.

Me, if it stood in my power, if it depended only on me to bring joy to the farm and change ways, I'd go straight up to Vulva and say: "It's true you've a pile of wrongs on your shoulders, but me, I'd like to start back like usual again, with the normal life and the marriage bed," and for sure Vulva would say "I agree," and she'd sleep in our bedroom in place of off by herself like she does now, chilly all the time with her feet freezing and her nose like an icicle.

But just it's not easy or simple like you'd fancy, for you've hardly made a move, hardly started stroking, when Vulva she turns awkward and goes all stiff, turning pages like she's never noticing a thing, or worse, threatening if you touch she'll make a complaint, so you're left like a jackass and it's a flop.

It's a pity, for by my reckoning she'd profit a whole lot if she let herself be approached and softened up and cuddled, especial for you know how much she likes it, and the notion comes to me that prideful she never gathers up to show the great longing she has, but for sure it'll soon come and she'll give in, and Paul he'll find her in his bed ready for surrender.

Right then she comes by to look at the flowers that's fading, and then she sits down on the bench to rest a while. She looks at the sky, she looks at the lanterns up in the leaves, and the young ones at the pond, but she never says a thing, for she still never shows a shred of her soul, and you never know if it's maybe she's fixed on the belly or she's off in the clouds and all you'd have to do is pinch her to bring her back to life on earth and for her to come round and be a good wife to us again.

It lights in me like a spark to keep her company and for once to sit with her in place of keeping away off in the shadows. So I sit myself down not far off and I watch a while how the wee ones set about drowning the insects that fly outside when night's coming down, with my back leaned against the seat: "How's it going?" I say, all re-laxed now the work's done, and for today there was nothing bad out of her that might have cast a cloud, except maybe she's not looking the way you'd like, eyes down, nose down, chin and mouth down, and her cheek hid behind her hair, when if she just put on a nice smile it would make a bit of a pleasant atmosphere. "What about a wee smile?" I go friendly putting a tenderness in my tone like I used before I found out, before she showed things was all gone sour inside and she was rotted deep down from not being an obliging wife.

Vulva, she turns away in the other direction, like to show it's an annoyance.

"Come now Vulva," I go, sliding up the bench, "what about a wee smile for Paul, your husband Paul," and the hand out of con-trol reaches out with not one scrap of sense and goes ferreting in the folds of the dress.

Vulva lifts the hand out and she says "No!" in a voice like a lady's, and she pulls off till she stands up out of fear I'm coming to yoke with her, and she goes round the corner against the wall, and now in the dark with so few lanterns the urge swells below to tumble her on her back right there in the grass and take my bit of pleasure and have some sport, for it's Saturday.

"Come on, come on," I order her taking her hands in mine, "it'll give you pleasure too," seeing since the party the hussy's never had any relations, and I grab her by the thighs till I can get between, and she shouts out, she bawls like a crazy one, calling for Georges, and when

I'm done I tell her "there," working her over on the breasts for her to know what they're good for and what she's good for on the farm, and anyway he's away a long time now and doesn't give a rat's fart.

Some of the young ones come peeking round the corner out of curiosity but I bark to get away, for of course they've already guessed the bawling's from Vulva and they're getting a good laugh. Anyway, you can't make out a thing in this pitch dark, so they can't see if Vulva has her skirt down or thrown over her head with the apron a wee bit torn and hair like a witch.

All the while I'm issuing them orders and getting up and tucking in my shirt I never notice she's crawled across on the ground like a snake to the hoe we leave outside, the one that's rusted from the rain and we never bother to put away, and then of course she lands me a clout on the leg with it, never harming me nor causing me much of a wound but a wicked clout all the same, though too low to damage anything vital, and she whales away at my calves and claws at my feet panting with rage till I say: "Quit that!" and I take the hoe from her, but the sow she pulls me by the leg and I fall flat, and she makes a grab at me, but I stop first, figuring there's no point giving her a licking, and out of upset at what took place, and it's piercing cold too.

In the kitchen the youngsters is in their places, it's almost quiet, it seems strange and it strikes you, them all quieted down that way. They reach out their plates and I dole the food Vulva warmed up, and I say: "No talking!" but I never shout when they try to start up their ruckus again.

34

Time comes to put away the tools we'll lay in their places for over winter, and then there's leisure to smoke two or three pipes in front of the stove and pamper the cows a bit more, and then comes the slurry and seeding the fields. Life's like that, a wheel that turns faster and more and more frequent all the time, so the seasons seem to pass quicker than they used.

I'm busy on my own in the shed, but never grudging: it's good to go at your own speed and reflect, and that way it's not hard to get ahead. I toil along silent as long as I never see the time and I never hear anyone coming, lost in my reflecting, so I give a jump when from the doorway a voice calls out.

It's one of the young ones comes forward and asks his pa for a talk. It's so rare one comes in and opens its trap to have a chat that I lay down the shaft, sure it's another time-waster of a quarrel between the young ones, and I go: "Yes?" not in a pleasant voice, not welcoming and kind like a son hopes for, but like a man disrupted from his work: "Yes?" I repeat. "What's so urgent, sonny?"

It comes out of me from deep-buried affection to say "sonny," so unexpected like that, not that I'd premeditated, but when one of them comes in to chat it sends a thrill of happiness deep through a father, and it shows up in the words, even if there's a dark mug and a forehead creased at the disturbance.

"So what's up then?" I say, waving for him to come, to come in out of the doorway, for I've eaten already so there's no chance I'll gobble him up, I say out of sport, but maybe the lad's scared for he's holding his lips pinched tight.

This young one, I know which it is, it's one of them we got early on, and maybe even the very first Vulva put on this earth, if I'm not mistook. He's one you can still recognize from his appearance, though they all have the same slyness of young monkeys in their mugs, but this one, I notice, you can look at him straight and never have to lower your nose, and even due to his boots maybe or the floor it almost seems you have to lift your head to look at him.

"What is it then?" I prod him, for he's standing still gawping with his hands in his pockets, and if he waits longer to speak I'll pick up the handle to get back at it, but then it comes out of him in a deep voice: he says the time to talk has come, and there's a lot needs to be said. He's had enough of being here treated like a kid, he says, this little lump of shit with you'd figure just a couple of hairs on his lip, it's time for him to leave after the business with Georges and now last evening, and you'd say he had square shoulders and maybe broader than mine, yes, it's time to go, but he's just short the money for the trip. I'm wondering about the armpits and chest and so on, and about a young one grown up already that wants his slice of the pie, and it cuts through me just when I'm saying: "You snot-nosed little good-for-nothing," and I haul back to land him a clout, but the brat he parries off and grabs me by the shoulder and sends me flying, for it's no surprise the young has more potent muscles. Before I can get back on my feet and take a run at him to teach respect, he's shouting in a man's voice already: "Shit!" and: "Asshole!" and maybe: "Bastard!" but not distinct, and by the time I'm out into the yard he's off with all his things packed on the moped, but it won't get farther than a couple of miles anyway before it dies on him, rotted like it is with the engine all tinkered over, near out of gas, and most of it rust.

It lands you like a punch in the gut all the same to see a youngster of your own, the fruit of your loins, taking off that way, and I'm rooted there flabbergasted watching this pup setting off on the hill, but it comes to me sudden that if I like I can drive the tractor after him and give him his licking; but with no money he'll not be gone for long, and anyway one less is no disaster to the farm, and I think of the shoulders and the couple of chin-hairs.

There's some grow up and mature and you never notice till they start figuring they're not young ones in short pants any more, and you can understand that, except if you're a man you have to sweat, you have to get started on things, you have to labor in the field or the cow barn. It's too easy to say "Pa, I'm grown-up, hand over some cash," and set off down the road before you've ever proved yourself and never earned it like a wage.

Me, a young one that grew up, that came to do its bit and was there beside me ready to sweat like you'd want, I'd hand him his money—maybe not the whole lot, but I'd hand over one or two coins now and then just to show his brothers you can grind away hard and at the same time be open-handed with your reapings.

Now the other young ones is standing in the yard like myself with their eyes pinned on the road, though he's long gone with neither hair nor hide of him in sight, nothing but the asphalt, and that upsets me, for what difference if one of the little whelps takes off, so I give them a telling off to let them know who it is has to work all the time, and as they head off scuffling against one another I take a good look at them and I can see there's lots will be grown up before you know it.

If you try to count them it's no easy job, seeing they're always shifting and never keep still, never obedient and ready to answer but roaming the fields poking under every blade of grass. When you come across one it's impossible to tell any more if it's the same as the last one, or a big brother, or if there's twins. All the same, there's some I know: there's the one with the creases dug by the disease, and the pitted one, though they might be the same; there's one has its Pa's nose—no winner that one—and the one that might as well be sick and still goes coughing from the angina, and then there's that female one that says nothing you can ever make out at first and that you overlook deliberate when you need a hand, for she's not worth the trouble and has no vigor in her, but still when the juices rise in her she'll turn a whole woman on us.

35

All right, so then there's the harrows to be cleaned up and brought in from where they've been lying outside all season, and so much to do there's no knowing what's most urgent. Fields after harvest, the land's left looking scraggy: the eye takes in wider and the earth looks turned again, but not virgin no more with the dry clumps and short stubble telling you it bore all its fruit a short while back.

It's the excuse to go the rounds, to step out across the land in this season I've to say I love better than spring, with the country-side waiting to be draped in snow. The land's still lovely and rich: here you can replant too, next year, and one day this ugly clump of trees can be cut down, and for sure none of them that want to save the rabbits will ever come demonstrating; from here if you twist your neck you can see the roof of the barn and a shed; in the field above, the machine always gets stuck on the rocks, so it's a wonder they can get up the slope at all, and it was right here Pa let out his "Ah!" and sat down on the ground, and I carried him on my back till I could lay him in bed in his room.

I halt a minute to honor his memory, seeing I never visit the grave often, and I lower my eyes a few minutes, like almost a prayer. When I look up there's one of the young ones on the hillside coming fast this way and yammering words no one could catch, so I go: "What?" letting him come and never even raising my voice. Every time you head off by yourself and leave the reins a bit slack it never fails but there's some panic on the farm, like as if without me the whole thing runs off track.

"Is the barn on fire then?" I go sarcastic from far, "Or maybe it's an earthquake?" The youngster's coming uphill and I've all my time to watch him. He's one of the ones I mix up, with never a hair on his chin yet, a younger of the ones that look alike, with his forehead dripping and his cheeks red like they was slapped.

"What's the matter then?" I ask when he comes in reach.

"Uh, uh . . . the cow . . . the cow . . ." he answers, so I shake him like a tree of ripe fruit, and at last he spits out the reason: there's one has fallen in her stall and they tried to get her up again but she won't stand straight on her legs.

"So what," I analyze, "she's just chewing her cud on us after a lag, it's normal they lie down when they've their bellies-full."

But no, it's not her cud, he says then, it's just the opposite: she drooled like something black and she's shaking in the legs sometimes, so she's sick for sure.

I wonder to myself how when they was in good shape this morning they can have found the time to deteriorate. All the same we go back at top speed, as fast as our legs can carry.

It seems it's Blossom.

When we get to the cow barn the doctor vet is already good and busy taking pulses and unpacking the bundles of herbs he's made his method: it's the latest thing, they say, and works fantastic on critters that's not closed-minded like some people. He's measuring her on the udder, he's taking his time prodding her, but even so afterwards he takes out his stethoscope, though he explains that normal he finds it old-fashioned, and he sounds her up to the four armpits.

In the end I get impatient and I say straight out maybe the cow she'll be dead before he's done, and a big laughing fit comes over me, but it's out of nerves. After he's been through the whole routine he prepares her his mixture and he slips three black pellets on her tongue for her to chew, and Blossom she chews.

Blossom's my favorite, for it's not true it's Codfish, it's Blossom I like best, now you can see she's all scared and trembling I can say you feel how close you is, you feel the wave of affection, and it comes over fond to say to her all tender: "Come now my sweet," and stroke her on the neck, and I'm just setting to reach out my hand when the vet stops me while he's counting out on his bag: we have to take care, he says, due to the contagion. Him, he explains with respect to my objection that if he can touch why not their master, it's normal he exposes himself, for he does it out of profession and principle, and he soaps down for a real long time after, but if I touch and all the others come down in consequence it's too big a risk.

From the bag of pellets she's supposed to get ten every day till she gets better, if she does. The vet hands me the sheet where he's written down the fee and then he clears off before I've time to ask him what sickness it is.

She's not the first one brought down by a sickness. Once already, long ago, long before Vulva came, long before the young ones and the vexations, when we was just two of us alone on this farm, and when we had no Brownie nor Jasmine but their mamas, and maybe even their grandmas, there was one died on the farm from some dirty sickness. Back then there was more chores than even now and no time for playing hospitals, so we sent for Jules with his gun and he shot a cartridge into her.

In them days you never recognized proper what an animal means, and maybe even you thought they're all of a muchness, that they're just horns, a belly, a tail, and above all a big udder that gives milk you can sell for good money. When you're young you never know anything, but Pa never felt a thing either, for deep inside his heart it was hard as stone.

"It's for Martine," we said, and then it was bang between the horns and we went back to our business never giving another thought except to have the body carted away.

It torments me thinking about Martine that's dead now from years back, how she never knew any affection and was left to die cruel alone on our straw, and terrible sick on top of it.

"What's wrong with Blossom?" they come bawling, the youngsters, and they're looking for a good licking, for a clout with the stick to calm them down and stop them careering around infecting the whole cow barn, but I just say: "Take care, don't touch!" hardly shouting at all, maybe out of weariness or old age looming sudden into life.

The next day it's the same, no heart for work and, what's strange, no heart for the breakfast cheese either, so I'm out in the field after ten by the wrist with my legs like jelly and dripping from the forehead.

By good luck there's the young ones that never lag far back of their pa. I call two of them up to go and fetch me bread, and I keep two with me for the boards, little snot-noses that maybe reckon there's no risk in getting close. We make good speed at the job, and on the stroke of twelve the tool goes down on the spot, and they go galloping off ahead, spurred by their empty bellies.

As for me it's in no hurry I make for the farmhouse for the mid-day meal where I know there's soup left from yesterday they all slurp up with never a word, and a loaf, while Vulva waits behind, now she's got into her head to go sobbing and sniffing for no rea-son and almost continuous.

Normal I'm drawn to thinking about the meals and telling my-self when the time comes: "It's come time for the soup again," and thinking: "Maybe she cooked that chicken," and imagining what maybe she's simmered up for us, Vulva, for when she puts her mind into it and involves herself she can still cook a great stew, there's no denying.

But passing the cow barn it's stronger than my will, I have to go in and find Blossom.

"Blossom," I whisper into the straw in the dark, and the old lady she sticks her neck through the bars.

Seeing her at a glance that way, you'd fancy she was healthy, stand-ing there in the stall in the half light, but Paul's experienced and able to recognize the signs, especial in the eyes that is weeping like from fe-ver. The poor lass has shifted and she's trying to lick the master's hand, except it leaves a slimy trail on the palm, like black stuff you'd say.

36

The vet came by with the herbs several times, much obliged, and he answered laconic, with a look that left you not knowing what to think, maybe it's serious or maybe not, for we have to wait till the substances develop in the organism.

Then they took Blossom away for the cremating.

Meantime on the straw others started sweating, vomiting, and convulsing, so without going near nor having them seen I could tell already before the vet confirmed that it was the same infection that set them all shaking.

"It doesn't look good," he just said, all curious.

It's easy to understand how going from one animal to the next to look after them in their stalls and shoveling out the dung you give them their little pat on the neck or a shove on the rump, never giving a thought, or with the youngsters in their romps throwing the hay about, or me attaching the machines to the teats, and at their udders I can't help giving their coats a little stroke.

That's how it was with the days going and the vet coming more and more often, till in the end we had to decide to pack them all off before they went down on us with the same disease all around and across the region, and that would mean trouble for sure, the vet said, due to my civil liability. Anyway, it's not the tragedy it seems, he said, seeing the insurance money would let me buy even more splendid specimens.

Yes, but there'll be no more Codfish.

There'll be no more Codfish, and it's a picture haunts me in the night, Codfish mooing out of the truck, all joyful and trusting with that zest they always get from new things, and seeming to say: "No hard feelings, Paul!" and "Goodbye, goodbye! goodbye!" never noticing down on the ground Paul is shaking and not able to believe what he's seeing with his own two eyes, if it's really his own herd he's watching trucked off to the knacker's, if it's really him, Paul the owner of this farm, Paul Vulva's husband, Paul that's daddy to the wee ones, Paul that's fed all the animals and is standing here now in his yard ready to pack them off to that place, or if maybe it's another person, or maybe a movie.

At the last the men just had to come to say they was all loaded up and it'd be over quick and clean as soon as they reached where it's done. They have to go out through the gate for the truck to take the road and go up the hill shaking like a coffin full of moos, so in the end you say but no one can hear: "Goodbye Codfish," for you're blubbering in the voice.

Mornings now the mist patches always linger on till late. Some-times there's a fog, and then you know you're stuck in the shed till near supper time, fixing whatever's in need of it.

There's some grow up bit by bit to like the work and take an interest in the whole business.

That takes time.

The insurance came, for signing the papers.

"Good morning Madame," they said, and she brought them in, and it was no use troubling your head to understand.

The barn roof needs fixing, but for that you need summer. Any-way, maybe we'll wait a couple of winters even, for never mind what the young ones say, it's not in real bad shape, and it'll be a while before it falls down round our heads.

In the woods we found logs in the piles they leave there with no watch ever kept on them. It'll always come in handy for the heat-ing. All the same we picked up some dead wood, with Vulva.

We can say we're well ready for winter and no mistake, for it to leave us reasonable in peace and quiet.

On the bench in front of the farmhouse it's good to warm yourself and catch the last of the sun, seeing December's coming under our noses.

Now the light's ending, it's time for a cup, with all the young ones off at school and just a pair of hens scratching and clucking away like usual, and the cock, and the cold from the wall behind creeping through your coat.

The cock he comes up close to my legs pecking at the gravel, one foot hooked off the ground, shinier in his feathers than the hen, a brighter, rusty red. He looks at me with his little starey black eye, eye to eye, proud, like it's the first time he's noticed me.

And then someone comes up and sits on the bench beside me, dressed in a green apron and a pair of old slippers, with broad hips spread out, setting herself down to get a little comfort from the autumn warmth and maybe her husband's as well, so I make the effort and set my burnt palm on her shoulder and leave it resting, and it means to say: "I'm pleased with you, wife."

NOËLLE REVAZ was born in 1968 in the canton of Valais, Switzerland. She is the author of short stories, plays, and a novel, *Efina*. Besides her work as a writer, she teaches creative writing at the Swiss Literature Institute at Biel/Bienne, where she lives.

W. DONALD WILSON is a professor at the University of Waterloo in Canada. He is a translator of fiction and nonfiction from the French and his work includes titles by Yves Thériault, Jean Heffer, and Jacques Chessex.

PETROS ABATZOGLOU, *What Does Mrs. Freeman Want?*
MICHAL AJVAZ, *The Golden Age.*
The Other City.
PIERRE ALBERT-BIROT, *Grabinoulor.*
YUZ ALESHKOVSKY, *Kangaroo.*
FELIPE ALFAU, *Chromos.*
Locos.
JOÃO ALMINO, *The Book of Emotions.*
IVAN ÂNGELO, *The Celebration.*
The Tower of Glass.
DAVID ANTIN, *Talking.*
ANTÓNIO LOBO ANTUNES, *Knowledge of Hell.*
The Splendor of Portugal.
ALAIN ARIAS-MISSON, *Theatre of Incest.*
IFTIKHAR ARIF AND WAQAS KHWAJA, EDS., *Modern Poetry of Pakistan.*
JOHN ASHBERY AND JAMES SCHUYLER, *A Nest of Ninnies.*
ROBERT ASHLEY, *Perfect Lives.*
GABRIELA AVIGUR-ROTEM, *Heatwave and Crazy Birds.*
HEIMRAD BÄCKER, *transcript.*
DJUNA BARNES, *Ladies Almanack.*
Ryder.
JOHN BARTH, *LETTERS.*
Sabbatical.
DONALD BARTHELME, *The King.*
Paradise.
SVETISLAV BASARA, *Chinese Letter.*
MIQUEL BAUÇÀ, *The Siege in the Room.*
RENÉ BELLETTO, *Dying.*
MAREK BIEŃCZYK, *Transparency.*
MARK BINELLI, *Sacco and Vanzetti Must Die!*
ANDREI BITOV, *Pushkin House.*
ANDREJ BLATNIK, *You Do Understand.*
LOUIS PAUL BOON, *Chapel Road.*
My Little War.
Summer in Termuren.
ROGER BOYLAN, *Killoyle.*
IGNÁCIO DE LOYOLA BRANDÃO, *Anonymous Celebrity.*
The Good-Bye Angel.
Teeth under the Sun.
Zero.
BONNIE BREMSER, *Troia: Mexican Memoirs.*
CHRISTINE BROOKE-ROSE, *Amalgamemnon.*
BRIGID BROPHY, *In Transit.*
MEREDITH BROSNAN, *Mr. Dynamite.*
GERALD L. BRUNS, *Modern Poetry and the Idea of Language.*
EVGENY BUNIMOVICH AND J. KATES, EDS., *Contemporary Russian Poetry: An Anthology.*
GABRIELLE BURTON, *Heartbreak Hotel.*
MICHEL BUTOR, *Degrees.*
Mobile.
Portrait of the Artist as a Young Ape.
G. CABRERA INFANTE, *Infante's Inferno.*
Three Trapped Tigers.
JULIETA CAMPOS, *The Fear of Losing Eurydice.*
ANNE CARSON, *Eros the Bittersweet.*
ORLY CASTEL-BLOOM, *Dolly City.*
CAMILO JOSÉ CELA, *Christ versus Arizona.*
The Family of Pascual Duarte.
The Hive.
LOUIS-FERDINAND CÉLINE, *Castle to Castle.*
Conversations with Professor Y.
London Bridge.
Normance.
North.
Rigadoon.
MARIE CHAIX, *The Laurels of Lake Constance.*
HUGO CHARTERIS, *The Tide Is Right.*
JEROME CHARYN, *The Tar Baby.*
ERIC CHEVILLARD, *Demolishing Nisard.*
LUIS CHITARRONI, *The No Variations.*
MARC CHOLODENKO, *Mordechai Schamz.*
JOSHUA COHEN, *Witz.*
EMILY HOLMES COLEMAN, *The Shutter of Snow.*
ROBERT COOVER, *A Night at the Movies.*
STANLEY CRAWFORD, *Log of the S.S. The Mrs Unguentine.*
Some Instructions to My Wife.
ROBERT CREELEY, *Collected Prose.*
RENÉ CREVEL, *Putting My Foot in It.*
RALPH CUSACK, *Cadenza.*
SUSAN DAITCH, *L.C.*
Storytown.
NICHOLAS DELBANCO, *The Count of Concord.*
Sherbrookes.
NIGEL DENNIS, *Cards of Identity.*
PETER DIMOCK, *A Short Rhetoric for Leaving the Family.*
ARIEL DORFMAN, *Konfidenz.*
COLEMAN DOWELL, *The Houses of Children.*
Island People.
Too Much Flesh and Jabez.
ARKADII DRAGOMOSHCHENKO, *Dust.*
RIKKI DUCORNET, *The Complete Butcher's Tales.*
The Fountains of Neptune.
The Jade Cabinet.
The One Marvelous Thing.
Phosphor in Dreamland.
The Stain.
The Word "Desire."
WILLIAM EASTLAKE, *The Bamboo Bed.*
Castle Keep.
Lyric of the Circle Heart.
JEAN ECHENOZ, *Chopin's Move.*
STANLEY ELKIN, *A Bad Man.*
Boswell: A Modern Comedy.
Criers and Kibitzers, Kibitzers and Criers.
The Dick Gibson Show.
The Franchiser.
George Mills.
The Living End.
The MacGuffin.
The Magic Kingdom.
Mrs. Ted Bliss.
The Rabbi of Lud.
Van Gogh's Room at Arles.
FRANÇOIS EMMANUEL, *Invitation to a Voyage.*
ANNIE ERNAUX, *Cleaned Out.*
SALVADOR ESPRIU, *Ariadne in the Grotesque Labyrinth.*
LAUREN FAIRBANKS, *Muzzle Thyself.*
Sister Carrie.
LESLIE A. FIEDLER, *Love and Death in the American Novel.*
JUAN FILLOY, *Faction.*
Op Oloop.
ANDY FITCH, *Pop Poetics.*
GUSTAVE FLAUBERT, *Bouvard and Pécuchet.*
KASS FLEISHER, *Talking out of School.*

FORD MADOX FORD,
The March of Literature.
JON FOSSE, *Aliss at the Fire.*
Melancholy.
MAX FRISCH, *I'm Not Stiller.*
Man in the Holocene.
CARLOS FUENTES, *Christopher Unborn.*
Distant Relations.
Terra Nostra.
Vlad.
Where the Air Is Clear.
TAKEHIKO FUKUNAGA, *Flowers of Grass.*
WILLIAM GADDIS, *J R.*
The Recognitions.
JANICE GALLOWAY, *Foreign Parts.*
The Trick Is to Keep Breathing.
WILLIAM H. GASS, *Cartesian Sonata*
and Other Novellas.
Finding a Form.
A Temple of Texts.
The Tunnel.
Willie Masters' Lonesome Wife.
GÉRARD GAVARRY, *Hoppla! 1 2 3.*
Making a Novel.
ETIENNE GILSON,
The Arts of the Beautiful.
Forms and Substances in the Arts.
C. S. GISCOMBE, *Giscome Road.*
Here.
Prairie Style.
DOUGLAS GLOVER, *Bad News of the Heart.*
The Enamoured Knight.
WITOLD GOMBROWICZ,
A Kind of Testament.
PAULO EMÍLIO SALES GOMES, *P's Three*
Women.
KAREN ELIZABETH GORDON, *The Red Shoes.*
GEORGI GOSPODINOV, *Natural Novel.*
JUAN GOYTISOLO, *Count Julian.*
Exiled from Almost Everywhere.
Juan the Landless.
Makbara.
Marks of Identity.
PATRICK GRAINVILLE, *The Cave of Heaven.*
HENRY GREEN, *Back.*
Blindness.
Concluding.
Doting.
Nothing.
JACK GREEN, *Fire the Bastards!*
JIŘÍ GRUŠA, *The Questionnaire.*
GABRIEL GUDDING,
Rhode Island Notebook.
MELA HARTWIG, *Am I a Redundant*
Human Being?
JOHN HAWKES, *The Passion Artist.*
Whistlejacket.
ELIZABETH HEIGHWAY, ED., *Contemporary*
Georgian Fiction.
ALEKSANDAR HEMON, ED.,
Best European Fiction.
AIDAN HIGGINS, *Balcony of Europe.*
A Bestiary.
Blind Man's Bluff
Bornholm Night-Ferry.
Darkling Plain: Texts for the Air.
Flotsam and Jetsam.
Langrishe, Go Down.
Scenes from a Receding Past.
Windy Arbours.
KEIZO HINO, *Isle of Dreams.*
KAZUSHI HOSAKA, *Plainsong.*

ALDOUS HUXLEY, *Antic Hay.*
Crome Yellow.
Point Counter Point.
Those Barren Leaves.
Time Must Have a Stop.
NAOYUKI II, *The Shadow of a Blue Cat.*
MIKHAIL IOSSEL AND JEFF PARKER, EDS.,
Amerika: Russian Writers View the
United States.
DRAGO JANČAR, *The Galley Slave.*
GERT JONKE, *The Distant Sound.*
Geometric Regional Novel.
Homage to Czerny.
The System of Vienna.
JACQUES JOUET, *Mountain R.*
Savage.
Upstaged.
CHARLES JULIET, *Conversations with*
Samuel Beckett and Bram van
Velde.
MIEKO KANAI, *The Word Book.*
YORAM KANIUK, *Life on Sandpaper.*
HUGH KENNER, *The Counterfeiters.*
Flaubert, Joyce and Beckett:
The Stoic Comedians.
Joyce's Voices.
DANILO KIŠ, *The Attic.*
Garden, Ashes.
The Lute and the Scars
Psalm 44.
A Tomb for Boris Davidovich.
ANITA KONKKA, *A Fool's Paradise.*
GEORGE KONRÁD, *The City Builder.*
TADEUSZ KONWICKI, *A Minor Apocalypse.*
The Polish Complex.
MENIS KOUMANDAREAS, *Koula.*
ELAINE KRAF, *The Princess of 72nd Street.*
JIM KRUSOE, *Iceland.*
AYŞE KULIN, *Farewell: A Mansion in*
Occupied Istanbul.
EWA KURYLUK, *Century 21.*
EMILIO LASCANO TEGUI, *On Elegance*
While Sleeping.
ERIC LAURRENT, *Do Not Touch.*
HERVÉ LE TELLIER, *The Sextine Chapel.*
A Thousand Pearls (for a Thousand
Pennies)
VIOLETTE LEDUC, *La Bâtarde.*
EDOUARD LEVÉ, *Autoportrait.*
Suicide.
MARIO LEVI, *Istanbul Was a Fairy Tale.*
SUZANNE JILL LEVINE, *The Subversive*
Scribe: Translating Latin
American Fiction.
DEBORAH LEVY, *Billy and Girl.*
Pillow Talk in Europe and Other
Places.
JOSÉ LEZAMA LIMA, *Paradiso.*
ROSA LIKSOM, *Dark Paradise.*
OSMAN LINS, *Avalovara.*
The Queen of the Prisons of Greece.
ALF MAC LOCHLAINN,
The Corpus in the Library.
Out of Focus.
RON LOEWINSOHN, *Magnetic Field(s).*
MINA LOY, *Stories and Essays of Mina Loy.*
BRIAN LYNCH, *The Winner of Sorrow.*
D. KEITH MANO, *Take Five.*
MICHELINE AHARONIAN MARCOM,
The Mirror in the Well.
BEN MARCUS,
The Age of Wire and String.

SELECTED DALKEY ARCHIVE TITLES

WALLACE MARKFIELD,
Teitelbaum's Window.
To an Early Grave.
DAVID MARKSON, *Reader's Block.*
Springer's Progress.
Wittgenstein's Mistress.
CAROLE MASO, *AVA.*
LADISLAV MATEJKA AND KRYSTYNA
POMORSKA, EDS.,
Readings in Russian Poetics:
Formalist and Structuralist Views.
HARRY MATHEWS,
The Case of the Persevering Maltese:
Collected Essays.
Cigarettes.
The Conversions.
The Human Country: New and
Collected Stories.
The Journalist.
My Life in CIA.
Singular Pleasures.
The Sinking of the Odradek
Stadium.
Tlooth.
20 Lines a Day.
JOSEPH MCELROY,
Night Soul and Other Stories.
THOMAS MCGONIGLE,
Going to Patchogue.
ROBERT L. MCLAUGHLIN, ED., *Innovations:*
An Anthology of Modern &
Contemporary Fiction.
ABDELWAHAB MEDDEB, *Talismano.*
GERHARD MEIER, *Isle of the Dead.*
HERMAN MELVILLE, *The Confidence-Man.*
AMANDA MICHALOPOULOU, *I'd Like.*
STEVEN MILLHAUSER, *The Barnum Museum.*
In the Penny Arcade.
RALPH J. MILLS, JR., *Essays on Poetry.*
MOMUS, *The Book of Jokes.*
CHRISTINE MONTALBETTI, *The Origin of Man.*
Western.
OLIVE MOORE, *Spleen.*
NICHOLAS MOSLEY, *Accident.*
Assassins.
Catastrophe Practice.
Children of Darkness and Light.
Experience and Religion.
A Garden of Trees.
God's Hazard.
The Hesperides Tree.
Hopeful Monsters.
Imago Bird.
Impossible Object.
Inventing God.
Judith.
Look at the Dark.
Natalie Natalia.
Paradoxes of Peace.
Serpent.
Time at War.
The Uses of Slime Mould:
Essays of Four Decades.
WARREN MOTTE,
Fables of the Novel: French Fiction
since 1990.
Fiction Now: The French Novel in
the 21st Century.
Oulipo: A Primer of Potential
Literature.
GERALD MURNANE, *Barley Patch.*
Inland.

YVES NAVARRE, *Our Share of Time.*
Sweet Tooth.
DOROTHY NELSON, *In Night's City.*
Tar and Feathers.
ESHKOL NEVO, *Homesick.*
WILFRIDO D. NOLLEDO, *But for the Lovers.*
FLANN O'BRIEN, *At Swim-Two-Birds.*
At War.
The Best of Myles.
The Dalkey Archive.
Further Cuttings.
The Hard Life.
The Poor Mouth.
The Third Policeman.
CLAUDE OLLIER, *The Mise-en-Scène.*
Wert and the Life Without End.
GIOVANNI ORELLI, *Walaschek's Dream.*
PATRIK OUŘEDNÍK, *Europeana.*
The Opportune Moment, 1855.
BORIS PAHOR, *Necropolis.*
FERNANDO DEL PASO, *News from the Empire.*
Palinuro of Mexico.
ROBERT PINGET, *The Inquisitory.*
Mahu or The Material.
Trio.
A. G. PORTA, *The No World Concerto.*
MANUEL PUIG, *Betrayed by Rita Hayworth.*
The Buenos Aires Affair.
Heartbreak Tango.
RAYMOND QUENEAU, *The Last Days.*
Odile.
Pierrot Mon Ami.
Saint Glinglin.
ANN QUIN, *Berg.*
Passages.
Three.
Tripticks.
ISHMAEL REED, *The Free-Lance Pallbearers.*
The Last Days of Louisiana Red.
Ishmael Reed: The Plays.
Juice!
Reckless Eyeballing.
The Terrible Threes.
The Terrible Twos.
Yellow Back Radio Broke-Down.
JASIA REICHARDT, *15 Journeys from Warsaw*
to London.
NOËLLE REVAZ, *With the Animals.*
JOÃO UBALDO RIBEIRO, *House of the*
Fortunate Buddhas.
JEAN RICARDOU, *Place Names.*
RAINER MARIA RILKE, *The Notebooks of*
Malte Laurids Brigge.
JULIÁN RÍOS, *The House of Ulysses.*
Larva: A Midsummer Night's Babel.
Poundemonium.
Procession of Shadows.
AUGUSTO ROA BASTOS, *I the Supreme.*
DANIËL ROBBERECHTS, *Arriving in Avignon.*
JEAN ROLIN, *The Explosion of the*
Radiator Hose.
OLIVIER ROLIN, *Hotel Crystal.*
ALIX CLEO ROUBAUD, *Alix's Journal.*
JACQUES ROUBAUD, *The Form of a*
City Changes Faster, Alas, Than
the Human Heart.
The Great Fire of London.
Hortense in Exile.
Hortense Is Abducted.
The Loop.
Mathematics:
The Plurality of Worlds of Lewis.

The Princess Hoppy.
Some Thing Black.
LEON S. ROUDIEZ, *French Fiction Revisited.*
RAYMOND ROUSSEL, *Impressions of Africa.*
VEDRANA RUDAN, *Night.*
STIG SÆTERBAKKEN, *Siamese.*
LYDIE SALVAYRE, *The Company of Ghosts.*
Everyday Life.
The Lecture.
Portrait of the Writer as a
Domesticated Animal.
The Power of Flies.
LUIS RAFAEL SÁNCHEZ,
Macho Camacho's Beat.
SEVERO SARDUY, *Cobra* & *Maitreya.*
NATHALIE SARRAUTE,
Do You Hear Them?
Martereau.
The Planetarium.
ARNO SCHMIDT, *Collected Novellas.*
Collected Stories.
Nobodaddy's Children.
Two Novels.
ASAF SCHURR, *Motti.*
CHRISTINE SCHUTT, *Nightwork.*
GAIL SCOTT, *My Paris.*
DAMION SEARLS, *What We Were Doing*
and Where We Were Going.
JUNE AKERS SEESE,
Is This What Other Women Feel Too?
What Waiting Really Means.
BERNARD SHARE, *Inish.*
Transit.
AURELIE SHEEHAN, *Jack Kerouac Is Pregnant.*
VIKTOR SHKLOVSKY, *Bowstring.*
Knight's Move.
A Sentimental Journey:
Memoirs 1917–1922.
Energy of Delusion: A Book on Plot.
Literature and Cinematography.
Theory of Prose.
Third Factory.
Zoo, or Letters Not about Love.
CLAUDE SIMON, *The Invitation.*
PIERRE SINIAC, *The Collaborators.*
KJERSTI A. SKOMSVOLD, *The Faster I Walk,*
the Smaller I Am.
JOSEF ŠKVORECKÝ, *The Engineer of*
Human Souls.
GILBERT SORRENTINO,
Aberration of Starlight.
Blue Pastoral.
Crystal Vision.
Imaginative Qualities of Actual
Things.
Mulligan Stew.
Pack of Lies.
Red the Fiend.
The Sky Changes.
Something Said.
Splendide-Hôtel.
Steelwork.
Under the Shadow.
W. M. SPACKMAN, *The Complete Fiction.*
ANDRZEJ STASIUK, *Dukla.*
Fado.
GERTRUDE STEIN, *Lucy Church Amiably.*
The Making of Americans.
A Novel of Thank You.
LARS SVENDSEN, *A Philosophy of Evil.*
PIOTR SZEWC, *Annihilation.*
GONÇALO M. TAVARES, *Jerusalem.*

Joseph Walser's Machine.
Learning to Pray in the Age of
Technique.
LUCIAN DAN TEODOROVICI,
Our Circus Presents . . .
NIKANOR TERATOLOGEN, *Assisted Living.*
STEFAN THEMERSON, *Hobson's Island.*
The Mystery of the Sardine.
Tom Harris.
TAEKO TOMIOKA, *Building Waves.*
JOHN TOOMEY, *Sleepwalker.*
JEAN-PHILIPPE TOUSSAINT, *The Bathroom.*
Camera.
Monsieur.
Reticence.
Running Away.
Self-Portrait Abroad.
Television.
The Truth about Marie.
DUMITRU TSEPENEAG, *Hotel Europa.*
The Necessary Marriage.
Pigeon Post.
Vain Art of the Fugue.
ESTHER TUSQUETS, *Stranded.*
DUBRAVKA UGRESIC, *Lend Me Your Character.*
Thank You for Not Reading.
TOR ULVEN, *Replacement.*
MATI UNT, *Brecht at Night.*
Diary of a Blood Donor.
Things in the Night.
ÁLVARO URIBE AND OLIVIA SEARS, EDS.,
Best of Contemporary Mexican Fiction.
ELOY URROZ, *Friction.*
The Obstacles.
LUISA VALENZUELA, *Dark Desires and*
the Others.
He Who Searches.
MARJA-LIISA VARTIO, *The Parson's Widow.*
PAUL VERHAEGHEN, *Omega Minor.*
AGLAJA VETERANYI, *Why the Child Is*
Cooking in the Polenta.
BORIS VIAN, *Heartsnatcher.*
LLORENÇ VILLALONGA, *The Dolls' Room.*
TOOMAS VINT, *An Unending Landscape.*
ORNELA VORPSI, *The Country Where No*
One Ever Dies.
AUSTRYN WAINHOUSE, *Hedyphagetica.*
PAUL WEST, *Words for a Deaf Daughter*
& *Gala.*
CURTIS WHITE, *America's Magic Mountain.*
The Idea of Home.
Memories of My Father Watching TV.
Monstrous Possibility: An Invitation
to Literary Politics.
Requiem.
DIANE WILLIAMS, *Excitability:*
Selected Stories.
Romancer Erector.
DOUGLAS WOOLF, *Wall to Wall.*
Ya! & John-Juan.
JAY WRIGHT, *Polynomials and Pollen.*
The Presentable Art of Reading
Absence.
PHILIP WYLIE, *Generation of Vipers.*
MARGUERITE YOUNG, *Angel in the Forest.*
Miss MacIntosh, My Darling.
REYOUNG, *Unbabbling.*
VLADO ŽABOT, *The Succubus.*
ZORAN ŽIVKOVIĆ, *Hidden Camera.*
LOUIS ZUKOFSKY, *Collected Fiction.*
VITOMIL ZUPAN, *Minuet for Guitar.*
SCOTT ZWIREN, *God Head.*